CASTLE OF TERROR

Nancy and George were about to head for the castle's dining room when they saw the grand duchess descending the staircase. Andrei and Emma were on either side of her.

Suddenly a maid rushed up the staircase, almost hysterical.

"Madam, you must come at once!" she cried. "The—the courtyard," the maid stammered. "The wall—"

Nancy and George followed Andrei, Emma, and the grand duchess as they trailed the sobbing maid downstairs and outside. The maid pointed to the bullet-pocked brick wall where, some fifty years earlier, eight Resistance fighters had been shot by the Nazis.

Nancy fought back a feeling of shock when she saw what had upset the maid. The wall was spattered with eight dark stains that ran down the bricks and pooled on the cobblestones.

"Blood!" George exclaimed, stunned.

Nancy Drew & Hardy Boys SuperMysteries

Available from ARCHWAY Paperbacks

A NANCY DREW and HARDY BOYS SUPER·MYSTERY™

EVIL IN AMSTERDAM

Carolyn Keene

AN ARCHWAY PAPERBACK
Published by POCKET BOOKS
New York   London   Toronto   Sydney   Tokyo   Singapore

This book is a work of fiction. Names, characters, places and incidents are either products of the author's imagination or are used fictitiously. Any resemblance to actual events or locales or persons, living or dead, is entirely coincidental.

AN ARCHWAY PAPERBACK *Original*

An Archway Paperback published by
POCKET BOOKS, a division of Simon & Schuster Inc.
1230 Avenue of the Americas, New York, NY 10020

Copyright © 1993 by Simon & Schuster Inc.
Produced by Mega-Books of New York, Inc.

ISBN: 0-671-78173-1

First Archway Paperback printing November 1993

10 9 8 7 6 5 4 3 2 1

NANCY DREW, THE HARDY BOYS, AN ARCHWAY PAPERBACK and colophon are registered trademarks of Simon & Schuster Inc.

NANCY DREW & HARDY BOYS SUPERMYSTERIES is a trademark of Simon & Schuster Inc.

Cover art by Alfons Kiefer

Printed in the U.S.A.

IL 6+

EVIL IN AMSTERDAM

Chapter

One

T HIS REMINDS ME of the area around River Heights," Nancy Drew said as the taxi from Schiphol Airport sped along the outskirts of the city of Amsterdam. "All these flat fields and suburbs—except for the windmills, it looks like parts of the Midwest."

Beside her, her good friend George Fayne nodded. "And except for all the dikes," she added. "I've never seen a field back home with dikes."

"Holland is surrounded by dikes to keep back the waters of the North Sea," their cab driver said in very good English. He was a middle-aged man with curly brown hair and a husky voice. "About half of our country is below sea level," he explained. "That is what *Netherlands* means—

1

'the low country.' There is an old saying here: God made the world, but the Dutch made Holland. Even Amsterdam is three meters below sea level."

"Three meters," Nancy echoed. "That's more than nine feet underwater."

The taxi driver laughed. "The dikes have held the water back for hundreds of years. I am certain they will not fail on your vacation."

"No problem," George said, winking at Nancy. "We're both pretty good swimmers."

The driver glanced quickly at the two Americans in the rearview mirror. His voice was suddenly serious. "The water of the North Sea is so cold, no human being can survive in it for more than three minutes."

"Maybe we *won't* go swimming," George said. "Besides, I'm sure Merissa has plans for us." Merissa Lang, who lived in Amsterdam, was George's friend. Nancy had never met Merissa, but George spoke of her often.

The cab entered the old city of Amsterdam, and Nancy suddenly felt as if she'd plunged three centuries back in time. Amsterdam was a city of narrow brick houses, anywhere from three to six stories high, with elaborately ornamented gables and red tile roofs. Built side by side along the ancient, murky canals, the buildings were so old that many were crooked and leaned into each other for support. The cobblestoned streets in front of the houses crossed the canals on small brick bridges.

Here and there, gray stone church towers rose above the red tile roofs, some with little gold steeples or delicate crowns. Others were tiny bell or clock towers. Everything was clean and prosperous looking, and the extremely narrow streets were filled with people riding battered but sturdy bicycles.

The driver stopped the cab in front of a tall, narrow townhouse on Oude Zijds Voorburgwal, a canal in the oldest part of Amsterdam, in a neighborhood called Nieuwe Markt. Merissa had explained in a letter to George that it was pronounced New Market—which was exactly what it meant, except that the towers of what had once been a gate in the city's wall were "new" almost six hundred years ago.

George glanced at the piece of paper she held in her hand. "This is it," she said. "Merissa's apartment should be on the fourth floor."

The two girls got out of the cab, took their suitcases from the trunk, and paid the driver.

"I wish Bess had been able to come with us," Nancy said as George rang the doorbell. Bess Marvin was George's first cousin, and the three friends had shared many adventures together.

George smiled. "Bess is in love. There was no way she was going to leave Kyle, even for a chance to go to Amsterdam." She rang the bell a second time. "And now Merissa is about to get married. I can't believe it. It seems like only a little while ago that we were kids playing together."

3

The girls shivered a little in the cold, damp wind. The gray, overcast sky seemed low and forbidding. The end of November did not have the best weather for visiting the Netherlands, but it was the only time Merissa could take off from her job to spend time with them.

Nancy stepped back on the cobblestoned street and gazed up at the old Dutch house. The date 1691 was inscribed in flowing letters on the fifth-floor gable, just below the red tile roof. Her eyes went to the fourth floor. There was no sign of life behind the delicate white lace curtains that hung in the windows.

"I don't understand," George said as she rang the bell for the third time. "Merissa promised she'd be here." She looked at her watch. "And we're even an hour and a half later than I told her. I'm sure that she wouldn't just go out. She'd wait for us."

"She was probably delayed," Nancy said. Merissa was a freelance reporter for the *International Tribune.* Since she had had an interview to do, she had been unable to meet them at the airport, but she had promised to be waiting at her apartment.

"Maybe the bell is out of order," George suggested. She pulled her wool scarf up over her short, dark hair and turned her back to the chilly wind. She looked up at the townhouse and shouted. "Merissa! Merissa! It's us!"

Almost immediately Nancy saw the lace curtains at a second-floor window stir. A face appeared, then disappeared. Suddenly the curtains parted again, and the window was flung open. A robust, middle-aged woman with streaks of gray in her dark brown hair peered out.

"Wat willen U?" she shouted in rapid Dutch. George and Nancy exchanged a quick glance. Neither could understand Dutch.

"We're looking for Merissa Lang," George called up in a tentative voice. "We're her friends."

The woman looked surprised. "From America?"

"Yes!" George shouted back.

The woman in the window disappeared behind the lace curtains without a word. Then her head popped out again. "Wait! I let you in," she said, her English lightly accented.

Nancy and George stood patiently at the door, both of them listening for footsteps inside. Instead, they heard a muffled thump behind the door.

Nancy looked at George. Then she pushed the wooden door lightly. It swung open, revealing a narrow hallway and a long steep staircase. But no one was there.

"Come! Come!" It was the voice of the woman who had been at the window. She was calling from upstairs. Nancy and George picked up their suitcases and entered the foyer.

Nancy's eyes flitted quickly around the dim interior. She noticed a rope stretched across one wall and going up the stairs. When she turned to see where it started, she discovered that it was attached to the bolt on the door. Nancy realized that when the rope was pulled, the latch opened. That was the thump they'd heard outside. Footsteps clumped on the stairs.

"Ach, that is typically Dutch," the woman said, appearing at the top of the first landing and seeing Nancy's eyes on the rope and latch. She walked halfway down. "I am Mevrouw—Mrs.—Wouters. I am the owner of this house—how do you say it?"

"Landlady?" Nancy suggested.

"Yes, that is it." Mevrouw Wouters nodded emphatically. "Merissa has told me her friends are coming."

"I'm George Fayne. This is my friend Nancy Drew," George said. "It's so unlike Merissa to forget."

"Merissa is always busy with her job, coming and going. And with a friend, too." Mevrouw Wouters looked at them knowingly. "He is very handsome and very rich, too, I think."

"That must be Andrei," George said to Nancy. She turned back to Mevrouw Wouters. "That's why we're visiting. They became engaged recently, and Merissa wants me to meet her fiancé."

The Dutch landlady brandished a key. "I will let you in to wait."

Carrying their bags, Nancy and George followed her up the staircase to Merissa's fourth-floor apartment. The stairs grew steeper as they climbed, and Nancy began to wish that she hadn't packed quite so much. By the time they ascended the last flight, the steps were almost as steep as a ladder leaning against a wall.

The wooden floorboards creaked loudly underfoot, and the old house smelled of plaster and ancient wood. Nancy couldn't help marveling that families had lived here for more than three hundred years.

"When was the last time you saw Merissa?" George asked Mevrouw Wouters when they stood on the tiny landing outside Merissa's door.

Mrs. Wouters inserted the key in the lock, then turned to George and pursed her lips. "Two, three days perhaps," she said dismissively. "But Merissa always tells me if she's going away, and she has said nothing. So I am sure she will be back very soon."

Mevrouw Wouters pushed the door open, revealing a cheerfully decorated apartment with simple modern furniture upholstered in brightly colored prints. White lace curtains hung at the large, old-fashioned windows.

The landlady left them, closing the door behind her. Nancy and George set their bags down in the living room. Nancy strode over to the windows and pushed aside the delicate lace. The living room overlooked the canal and the cobblestoned street.

George sank into the couch and heaved a disappointed sigh. "Not much of a welcoming party." She picked up a photograph in a silver frame from the side table. In it, a handsome

7

young man in his early twenties had his arm around Merissa's shoulder. They were both laughing.

"This must be Prince Andrei," she said.

"A *prince?*" Nancy said, turning from the window. "You told me he was rich and lived in a castle, but you didn't tell me he was royalty."

"Merissa says he's very casual about it. She specifically said we're to call him Andrei, not Your Royal Highness or anything like that."

"What else has she told you about him?" Nancy asked. Walking back to the center of the living room, she noticed a vase of tulips on a credenza, next to the television. They were drooping, and petals had fallen on the polished wood.

"He's got something Merissa calls old-world charm," George reported. "He's been treating her royally. He flew her to Paris for lunch, took her skiing in Switzerland, and gave her a sapphire pendant that she told me she wears all the time."

"No diamond ring?" Nancy teased.

George rolled her eyes. "Merissa said it's been ordered from Cartier, but according to her last letter, it hadn't arrived yet."

As George was talking, Nancy gazed around the living room and glanced into the kitchen. There was another vase of flowers on the table, also dead for at least several days. Strange, Nancy thought, frowning slightly.

"What's the matter?" George asked, seeing the

expression on Nancy's face. "I can tell when you're sleuthing." Nancy was a well-known amateur detective and seemed to attract mysteries the way a magnet attracts iron filings.

Nancy shrugged. "Probably nothing," she said. "I just wondered why these dead flowers haven't been thrown away."

"Merissa probably didn't have a chance to clean up before we got here," George said. "She works really hard."

"I'm sure you're right," Nancy said, but she couldn't stop herself from looking around. She walked into the kitchen and opened the refrigerator, which was only half as high as American ones and fit under the counter. She took out a carton of milk and sniffed at it. "Sour," she said. "And there's something here that looks like a science project. I think it was salad once."

George frowned. "I'm sure there's a reasonable explanation. A lot of people forget to throw out things from their refrigerators." She walked to the bedroom at the back of the apartment. Nancy was right behind her. Heavy drapes covered the windows, throwing the room into partial darkness. Nancy flung the drapes aside. Windows, securely bolted, overlooked a courtyard filled with sheds and little gardens.

George flicked on the overhead light to dispel the gloom. The room contained a bed, neatly made, and a desk, tidy and clear of everything except a blotter, a jar filled with pens, a telephone answering machine, and a laptop computer.

"Everything looks okay . . ." George began.

Nancy didn't say anything but pointed to a dresser between the desk and the window. The surface was covered with Merissa's earrings, bracelets, and necklaces. Most of it was costume jewelry, but a sparkling sapphire pendant rested in a blue velvet box.

George picked up the necklace. "This must be the pendant that Andrei gave her," she said. "I can't believe she'd go out and just leave it lying here like this, especially after telling me she wears it everywhere."

Nancy glanced at the answering machine—a zero in its display indicated no messages, but she tried pressing the buttons anyway. All she got was Merissa's prerecorded outgoing message.

Suddenly Nancy put her fingers to her lips and said, "Shhh!"

They heard footsteps on the stairs. Someone was approaching the door.

As a key turned in the lock, George turned to Nancy and said excitedly, "She's here!" With Nancy right behind her, George hurried to the door. She turned the handle and opened it, then jumped back in alarm and shock.

A tall, well-built man, wearing a long black cape and holding a leering white Harlequin mask over his face, leapt menacingly into the apartment!

Chapter

Two

Geography CHOKED BACK a scream. Nancy assumed a self-defense position, ready to counter-attack. The intruder jumped back, and behind the mask his gray eyes appeared as shocked as the girls'.

"Who are you?" Nancy and George demanded simultaneously.

The man in the cape paused. He bowed deeply and gracefully. "Andrei Romanov–von Baden," was his dignified reply. As he rose he removed the mask, revealing the same handsome, chiseled face the girls had seen in the photograph. He smiled warmly and shucked off the black cape. Beneath it, he was wearing a beautifully cut suit and a silk scarf. A gold signet ring with an enamel

11

coat of arms glinted on the fourth finger of his right hand.

"You must be Merissa's friends from America," he said.

Nancy and George introduced themselves.

"I'm terribly sorry to burst in on you like this," he murmured, glancing solicitously at them, clearly eager to make sure they were all right. He held up the mask. "I expected Merissa to be here. We went to a masked ball last week, and I wore this. I'm returning the mask and cape to the costume rental. I certainly didn't plan to shock anyone." He brightened. "And where is Merissa? Has she gone out?"

George explained that Merissa had not yet shown up.

"She's probably on a story," Andrei said. "When she is working on deadline, Merissa loses track of everything else." Then he noticed the dead flowers. "I sent those to her five days ago, just before I left for Switzerland," he murmured.

"When did you see her last?" George asked.

"About six days ago," the prince replied. "She came to the castle for dinner and stayed overnight in one of the guest rooms. I drove her back to Amsterdam the next morning on my way to the airport."

He faced Nancy and George, a reassuring expression on his face. "I'm certain Merissa was called away suddenly on an assignment for the *Tribune,*" he told them. "It wouldn't be the first time. I have some errands to run in Amsterdam today, so I'll stop by the *Tribune*'s offices and find out."

He handed them the keys he'd used to enter the building and the apartment. "Take these in case you need to go out. I'll ring the bell when I come back." He smiled again and added, "Of course, Merissa will probably be back before then."

"He *is* charming," Nancy said when Andrei had left. "Not to mention gorgeous. I can see why Merissa is in love with him."

"Mmm," George agreed in a distracted tone.

Nancy studied her friend with concern. She, George, and Bess had been friends for years. Together they had solved some of Nancy's most difficult cases. Besides being a good friend, George was a natural athlete who rarely panicked or let danger scare her. But now she was sitting in Merissa's apartment, looking very worried.

"It's just so unlike her," George said. "Next to you, Nan, Merissa is the most thorough person I've ever known. She'd never forget we were arriving today. And despite what Andrei said, she's always on time."

"I'm sure there's an explanation for all this," Nancy said. She knew that she was partially responsible for causing George to feel concerned. Perhaps, Nancy thought, her instincts were working overtime. Give it a rest, Drew, she ordered herself. "Look, why don't I rummage around in the kitchen and make some tea," Nancy offered.

"Andrei will be back in a while," she said, quickly adding, "if Merissa doesn't get back first."

Nancy went to the kitchen, took the kettle from the gas stove, and held it under the tap. She lit the gas burner and found some tea bags in the cupboard. A few minutes later Nancy and George were seated in easy chairs by the living room window, gazing out at the canal beyond and sipping tea. Finally George yawned. "I'm jet-lagged and I can barely keep my eyes open," she said. "I'm taking a nap."

George stretched out on Merissa's bed while Nancy stayed in the easy chair by the living room window. Occasionally long, flat barges moved slowly along the canal, leaving in their wake an iridescent rainbow slick of oil on the dark brown water. Then a glass-roofed tour boat went by, filled with a handful of late-season visitors.

Nancy awoke to the sound of the doorbell ringing. The room was nearly dark. She glanced at her wristwatch. It was four-thirty in the afternoon. She had drifted off for several hours. Outside, the sun had already set, and the street lamps were on, casting their lemon yellow light over the damp street and the old brick houses. She reached over and turned on a table lamp. There was still no sign of Merissa.

The doorbell rang again, this time more insistently. Nancy noticed a small circular mirror attached to the frame outside the window. It had been angled to reflect the front doorstep four stories below. A tall man in a dark coat was ringing the bell. Prince Andrei, Nancy realized. He must have put on the coat after he returned the cape, she thought. Nancy turned the window latch and pushed it open. "Just a minute! I'll come down!" she called.

Andrei waved and cupped his gloved hands to his mouth. "Just pull the rope!"

Nancy went to the apartment door. In the tiny hallway outside, she saw the rope that led along the wall and through the floor to the latch four stories below. She tugged on it and felt it give. A moment later Andrei's footsteps sounded on the stairs.

George came to the open front door, rubbing the sleep from her eyes. "Is Merissa back?"

Just then Andrei appeared on the steps. Nancy noticed that he looked grim. When he got to the top of the stairs, he asked anxiously, "Has Merissa returned?"

"You mean you haven't found her?" George asked, giving him back his keys.

Andrei took them with a nod of thanks. "At the *Tribune* office they told me it's possible Merissa is researching a story in the south of Holland," he said. "She was working on several projects at once."

"In other words, they don't know," George stated, glancing at Nancy.

Andrei shrugged. "She *is* a free-lancer, so she

often doesn't go by the office for days at a time. She was there three days ago, though, and mentioned she was working on a story."

"About what?" Nancy asked.

Andrei shook his head. "She didn't say. But apparently she was very excited about it."

"Now what do we do?" George asked Nancy. Before her friend could answer, Prince Andrei raised his index finger. "If I could make a suggestion, perhaps."

Nancy and George fell silent and looked at him.

"You shouldn't have to spend your first night here in an empty apartment. My grandmother has asked me to invite you to the castle for dinner."

"Castle?" Nancy echoed.

Andrei smiled. "It's only a short drive from Amsterdam, on the River Vecht. I live there with my grandmother and Emma, my younger sister."

"But what if Merissa comes back while we're gone?" George asked.

"We'll leave a note," Andrei said. "And I can send a car for her. Please. I would be honored to be your host until we hear from Merissa. She would want me to."

Nancy looked around at the apartment. With Merissa so clearly gone, it seemed bleak. She knew that if they spent the evening there, she and George would just be wondering where Merissa was.

"I don't know," George said doubtfully.

16

Nancy turned to her friend. "Why don't we accept Andrei's invitation?" she suggested. "It'll be fun, and probably, Merissa will call before dinner's over."

George sighed. "I guess so," she said, still reluctant.

"If she's not back by morning, we will talk to the police," Andrei assured them. "But I don't think it will be necessary. Besides," he continued, smiling, "one doesn't turn down a dinner invitation from the Grand Duchess Anna Sergeyevna Romanov."

Andrei pulled a gold pen from his breast pocket and quickly wrote a note for Merissa on a pad near the kitchen telephone. Downstairs, a gleaming red Porsche C 2 coupe was parked on the narrow cobblestoned street. Soon Nancy and George were speeding through the narrow streets of Amsterdam, to a castle on the River Vecht.

In New York City, in a time zone six hours earlier than in the Netherlands, Frank and Joe Hardy stepped into an elevator in the World Trade Center, in lower Manhattan.

Built like a football player, blond-haired Joe carried a bulky suitcase in each hand. He hoisted them across the elevator's threshold. The doors slid smoothly shut behind them.

Frank, at eighteen the older of the brothers by a year, glanced at the address written on the slip of paper in his hand. He pressed the button for the eighty-first floor.

"Here. You can have your suitcase back," Joe said, dropping one of the bags next to Frank. "Next time I'll navigate and you can be the beast of burden. It must weigh ninety pounds."

Frank, who was dark-haired and a little taller than Joe, had more of a swimmer's build. He glanced innocently at Joe as the elevator began its rapid ascent up one of the world's tallest buildings. "Joe, you bench-press twice that weight. What's the difference?"

"The difference is I like lifting weights at the gym. I hate carrying your suitcase. What's so heavy in it, anyway? Dad told us to pack for just four or five days."

Fenton Hardy, Frank and Joe's father, was an internationally renowned private detective. Over the years Frank and Joe had gotten involved in their own mystery cases and racked up an excellent success rate. Sometimes Mr. Hardy relied on his sons to help him out on his own assignments.

A day earlier Frank and Joe had arrived home from their Bayport high school, primed to start their Thanksgiving vacation. Instead, their aunt Gertrude gave them a message from their father, instructing them to meet him at the United States Treasury Department offices in New York City at ten o'clock the next morning.

"Some books," Frank said vaguely. "I thought I'd get a head start on that science paper that's due in a couple of weeks."

Joe looked shocked. "You brought homework?"

"Sure. We might have some time to kill."

"Yeah, right," Joe snorted. "Where do you think Dad's sending us?" he wondered. "Maybe London? Paris? Rome? Acapulco? Yes, the beach!"

Frank couldn't help grinning at his brother's fantasies. "Dad told us to bring our passports, so it must be out of the country. But for all we know, it could be the Siberian tundra. And knowing Dad . . ."

Joe nodded, suddenly a little apprehensive. "You're right. It could be anywhere."

The elevator stopped, and the doors slid silently open, revealing a large, bright reception area. They stepped out and identified themselves to the receptionist, who led them into a conference room where a long, polished rosewood table took up most of the space. Floor-to-ceiling windows looked out over New York harbor and the soaring skyscrapers of downtown Manhattan.

Fenton Hardy rose to greet his two sons. The tall, dark-haired detective motioned to the man who sat on the other side of the table. "Frank and Joe, I'd like you to meet Treasury Agent Eddie Drecker. Have a seat."

Frank and Joe set down their suitcases, shook hands with Agent Drecker, then pulled out chairs. Mr. Hardy nodded slightly at Drecker. The Treasury agent snapped open an expensive leather briefcase. He took out two metal bars, each almost half a foot long and several inches high and deep. They were a dull yellow color.

"Gold bullion!" Frank exclaimed softly.

"You got that right." Drecker nodded. He pushed the bars across the table.

"Have a look at the stamp on each bar," Fenton instructed.

Frank and Joe examined the bars carefully. Each had an identical stamp: the letters *BN,* with a small coat of arms beneath it. Beside it, also stamped into the gold, was a seven-digit number. The two numbers were different.

"BN stands for Bank Nederland," Drecker explained. "It's stolen gold."

"Stolen around fifty years ago," their father added.

Frank set down the bar he was holding. "What's this all about?"

Fenton Hardy cleared his throat. "I've been working on this case for the Treasury Department for several months now. We're cooperating with the Dutch government, and we finally have a breakthrough."

"So you want us to help," Joe guessed.

Fenton Hardy suppressed a smile. "In a way, yes." Then his eyes narrowed. "But in a very limited way. You and Frank are *not* being asked to solve this case. We need you to help us set up a sting to catch some criminals."

"No problem," Joe said. "Who do you want us to nab?"

Treasury Agent Drecker's eyes glinted with good humor. He nodded slightly at Mr. Hardy. "Why don't you brief them?"

The private detective looked at his sons. "During the Second World War, the Netherlands—the country we usually call Holland—was invaded and occupied by the Nazi armies. Near the end of the war, in 1944, the country was in total chaos. A huge shipment of gold that belonged to the Dutch bank was stolen."

"By persons unknown," Drecker added. "Probably by Nazi soldiers. And they killed eight people, Resistance fighters, doing it."

Fenton Hardy picked up one of the gold bars and pointed to the seven-digit number stamped on it. "That's a registration number. Each bar is marked, so it's readily identifiable. These two bars came from the stolen shipment."

"Wow," Frank murmured, staring at the bars. It was hard to believe the stolen gold had resurfaced after so many years. "I guess whoever stole it has been cashing it in."

"We think so," his father said. "Of course, others may have gotten their hands on it, but the gold has always surfaced according to a pattern. Periodically over the last fifty years some of the stolen gold has been identified, mixed in with large shipments of gold bars from other origins. Clearly, someone is secretly 'infiltrating' the gold into the international market for cash."

"That's why the United States Treasury hired your father," Drecker told them. "Previous investigations by the Dutch were never able to trace the origin of the 'infiltrated' gold bars."

"In the past few months," Fenton added, "two

more of the stolen ingots were found—these two. This time they were in a shipment heading from Europe to Fort Knox." Fenton gestured toward Drecker. "That's why the Treasury got involved."

Drecker leaned forward at the table and spoke earnestly to Frank and Joe. "We asked your father to trace every transaction where the stolen gold had turned up for the last fifty years to find a common link. And he did."

Joe grinned. "Way to go, Dad!"

"What was the link?" Frank asked.

"A bullion brokerage firm in Amsterdam," Fenton said. "Owned by a man named Johannes Appel."

"He's the crook?" Joe speculated.

Fenton Hardy shook his head. "I doubt it. I think he acts as a front man."

"You mean he's selling the gold for whoever stole it," Frank said.

Fenton nodded. "That's about it. But we're working with Dutch agents on a plan to trap him—and hope to trick him into revealing who does have the stolen gold bars."

Agent Drecker reached into the briefcase again. He took out two envelopes with an airline's logo on them and handed them to Frank and Joe. "Round-trip tickets to Amsterdam and your hotel reservations." Then Drecker withdrew a thick brown envelope and pushed it across the table. "And some documents for Mr. Appel."

"That's it?" Frank asked, picking up the envelope.

"That's it," his father confirmed. "Your cover story is that you're couriers for a New York investment house that has some gold bullion it wants to sell. The documents give him the details of the phony deal. After you deliver them, if you want to spend your Thanksgiving vacation in Holland, that's up to you."

"What about Appel? Doesn't he get arrested?" Joe demanded.

"That's not your business—" Drecker started to say.

Fenton Hardy signaled him to be silent. He turned to his sons. "The Dutch authorities will get Appel when they're good and ready. But we want the real culprits, the ones who stole the gold fifty years ago."

"What makes you think they're still alive?" Joe asked.

"We don't know for certain," Mr. Hardy answered. "We're working on tips from the Dutch government. But so far there's every indication that they are still alive, which means I don't want either of you getting involved beyond delivering these documents. It's too dangerous. Whoever the thieves are, they're ruthless. They killed to steal the gold. And they'll kill to keep it, too."

Chapter

Three

I CAN'T BELIEVE how dark it is already," Nancy said to Andrei as she and George rode with him in his Porsche to the castle. For the third time she checked her seat belt to make sure it was securely fastened: Andrei was driving way too fast for comfort.

"Yes, it's true," Andrei said. "We are much farther north than your home in America, so in winter our nights are very long. But in summer our days are long, too."

A half-moon glowed through the clouds of an overcast sky, giving some dim illumination to the countryside. They were driving through farmland—broad, flat fields surrounded by wide ditches that were filled with water. Old farms and the stone gates of country houses lined the road on one side. On the other ran the River Vecht, which was barely wider than a small stream. Far across the fields Nancy could barely make out the silhouettes of several old windmills.

"This farmland was surrounded by dikes and reclaimed from the sea hundreds of years ago," Prince Andrei explained. "The windmills were used to pump water out. Most of them still work, but now the Dutch use electric pumps."

"Do you really live in a castle?" George asked from the backseat of the Porsche.

The prince smiled. "Yes, I really do live in a castle. Just a small castle, but a real one, almost eight hundred years old. Of course, it has all the modern conveniences."

"I suppose your family has lived there for hundreds of years," Nancy speculated.

"Oh, no," Andrei said quickly. "My sister, Emma, and I have always lived in the castle. It was built by a Dutch prince centuries ago, but my family has owned it only since the Russian Revolution, in 1918, when they fled from St. Petersburg. My grandmother is a grand duchess. Of course, she was only a little girl then."

"You're actually Russian?" Nancy asked.

"Romanov–von Baden," Andrei repeated his last name. "My sister and I are half Russian and half German. Many members of the aristocracy in those two countries came to Holland when Russia and Germany became republics. My father and grandmother are Romanovs. My mother was a von Baden, a German princess."

"Do they live at the castle?" George asked.

Andrei glanced quickly back at her, a brief but sad smile flickering across his handsome face. "No, my parents were killed in an automobile accident when I was a young boy. Emma and I have lived with our grandmother ever since."

"I'm sorry," George said sincerely.

"That was so many years ago," Andrei said. "My grandmother and Emma and I make a very good family together. There—look up the road where those woods are. In a moment you will see the castle."

Nancy peered through the windshield. It had started to rain a little, and drops spattered the glass. She made out several acres of dense trees on the other side of the narrow river, a small forest surrounded by fields. As the Porsche approached the castle, Nancy caught a glimpse of light flickering between the trees. A moment later they were driving alongside the forest. Through the gaunt outlines of trees Nancy saw lights in several windows, then the dark outline of great square walls and the crenellated tops of several high towers.

Andrei braked the Porsche almost to a crawl as they drove across a narrow brick bridge that arched delicately over the river. On the other side, immense stone posts crowned with carved griffins stood on either side of a drive. The wide iron gates were open, but a man stood in the drive, blocking their way.

Andrei stopped the car, and the man approached. Nancy saw that he was middle-aged, with salt-and-pepper hair and a face creased by hard work and weathered by a life spent outdoors, she thought. He wore workman's clothing and knee-high rubber boots.

"It's the groundskeeper," Andrei explained quickly to Nancy and George. "His name is Ot Schrijver—a very Dutch name."

The prince rolled down his window. "Hello, Ot," he said. "I have some guests for dinner."

The groundskeeper stooped to look at Prince Andrei and nodded, his face impassive. His eyes floated across the driver's seat as he sought out the car's other passengers. Nancy saw him giving her a cold, suspicious look.

"Welcome, sir," Schrijver said in a gruff voice. "The grand duchess has been waiting."

The high-walled castle was made of red brick and surrounded by a water-filled moat. Andrei drove through the open gates and across a wooden drawbridge into a cobblestoned courtyard. Diamond-paned windows glittered warmly with light, revealing glimpses of a rich interior.

Andrei pulled his car up to a grand entrance, where stairs led up to enormous wooden doors. Almost immediately they opened, and a servant emerged. Andrei stepped from his car while the servant hurried down the steps and opened Nancy's door, then George's.

"Please," Andrei said, motioning toward the open castle doors. Nancy caught a glimpse of a fire burning in a huge hearth inside.

They walked through the doors and stepped into a grand, baronial hall with a high-beamed ceiling. Waves of welcoming heat radiated from a stone fireplace on one wall. Straight-backed wooden chairs lined the walls beneath oil portraits of men in stiff, old-fashioned collars.

George craned her neck and gazed up at the ceiling, where thick wood beams caught the firelight's glow. She looked back at Andrei and grinned. "Not a bad place to call home."

"Andrei!"

Nancy turned to see a girl who looked about sixteen run through a doorway at the end of the hallway. She had long, perfectly straight blond hair and wide, high cheekbones. She was wearing a blue wool skirt that went to her knees, and a white silk blouse.

"Emma!" Andrei cried, throwing his arms wide to greet her. "These are Merissa's friends." He introduced Nancy and George. "And this is my sister, Princess Emma."

Emma smiled warmly, her cornflower blue eyes sparkling. "Please, just Emma. I'm so glad to know you," she said in flawless English. "I love meeting people from America!"

"We're glad to meet you, too, Emma." Nancy smiled, taking an instant liking to the younger girl. "We just wish we knew where Merissa was."

Emma and Andrei's eyes quickly met before Emma turned back to Nancy and George. "Andrei telephoned and told Grandmama. I'm sure Merissa must be in the south of Holland researching a story, just as the people at her office said."

"I certainly hope so," George said.

"Grandmama is in the library," Emma told Andrei. She slipped her arm through Nancy's. "You must come so we can introduce you. And then we'll all have dinner together. Oh, I do want to ask you about America. I've never been there, and I'm—how do you say it?—dying to visit."

They walked from the great hall into an adjacent room, almost as large, where a wide staircase of elaborately carved dark brown wood rose to the second floor. Emma led them upstairs and down a long corridor, chattering and asking Nancy all kinds of questions about the United States. By the time they reached the end of the long hall, Andrei wore a bemused smile from his sister's excitement.

"You would think that my sister had never met a foreigner before," he commented.

Emma wrinkled her brow and gave her brother a cross look. "Well, hardly ever. I'm always cooped up at this castle like a bird in a cage," she said, pouting a little.

"Aren't you in school?" Nancy inquired.

Emma shook her head, looking almost regretful. "No, I have a tutor. She comes to the castle." A mischievous smile crossed the young princess's face. "This week she is home with the flu."

"You speak perfect English," George commented.

"Thank you!" Emma said. "Not perfect yet, but I am trying very hard."

They stopped at a pair of tall, paneled doors, flanked by two shoulder-high French porcelain vases. Andrei turned the gold handles and pushed the doors open.

The brightly lit room was almost forty feet long and lined floor to ceiling with books along one wall. There were exquisite marble fireplaces at each end, also surrounded by bookcases, and along the fourth wall was a row of tall windows with rich brocade drapes. Sofas and antique chairs had been arranged in three conversational groupings around the room.

Nancy saw a diminutive, white-haired woman at one of the windows straighten quickly, revealing an antique telescope. She turned to greet the newcomers.

"Grandmother!" Andrei said, smiling broadly. "These are Merissa's friends. Nancy Drew and George Fayne, the Grand Duchess Anna Sergeyevna Romanov."

The elderly woman strode forward, her step firm. Her hair was snow white and pulled back in a severe bun, and she wore a long, old-fashioned black dress that fell to just above her ankles. An antique cameo brooch was pinned to her collar. She appeared to be in her late seventies or early eighties. Still, her ice blue eyes as she examined Nancy and George were sharp. She gave them both a warm smile, stretched out her hands, and took George's between them.

"When Andrei told me you'd arrived with no sign of Merissa, I insisted that you be our guests this evening," she said in a strong voice. "Amsterdam is much too dour at this time of year to be there without a friend."

The prince's gray eyes twinkled. "My grandmother is a very insistent woman," he said.

"And I'm certain Merissa has only been delayed," the grand duchess said to Nancy and George. "Undoubtedly some modern technological mishap with an airplane schedule. I am delighted that you have agreed to join us for dinner."

"Thank you," George said.

Nancy nodded her thanks as well. After all, Nancy thought, echoing Andrei's remark, one didn't turn down an invitation from the Grand Duchess Anna Sergeyevna Romanov.

Joe Hardy peered out the airplane window as the jumbo jet began its final descent over Amsterdam. The sun had barely risen above the eastern horizon, casting a reddish glow across the earth that tilted below at an odd angle to the descending plane.

"You can see the entire city," Joe said, nudging Frank, who sat in the next seat.

"Oomph!" Frank blinked his eyes open and sat up. "What's up?"

"We're there, old buddy," Joe said.

"You had to wake me up for that?" Frank complained. He'd managed to sleep for most of the transatlantic flight, and as far as he was concerned, his nap could have lasted until they had taxied up the runway.

Joe ignored his brother's comment. "It's shaped sort of like a horseshoe."

"What?" Frank asked, shaking his head to clear it of sleep.

"Amsterdam. Look down there." Joe pressed back in his seat so Frank could look across him and out the window. Below the airplane a city of red tile roofs spread across the earth, the houses following concentric semicircles of canals that led from a wide river.

"It's just like the guidebook describes it," Joe continued. "Starting about eight hundred years ago, they built dikes to hold back the sea, and canals to drain the land. The first canals were semicircles, and as Amsterdam grew bigger and bigger, the people kept adding more canals around the old ones."

"Save your history lesson for after lunch." Frank sighed. He leaned back in his seat and closed his eyes again.

Almost an hour later, after landing and going through customs, Frank was wide awake. The Hardys took a taxi from Schiphol Airport to the Hotel Doelen, a big old brick building that rose above the canal in the old part of the city.

Joe was the first into their hotel room, where he instantly threw himself down on one of the two double beds. "It's about two o'clock in the morning American time. I could use some sleep."

Frank looked disgruntled. "I thought you slept on the airplane."

"Well, I tried. But that blond flight attendant kept walking up and down the aisle."

Frank laughed. "And you couldn't bear to close your eyes and not watch her."

Joe looked sheepish. He shrugged. "What can I say? I like blonds. And brunettes. And—"

"And we have work to do," Frank said, holding up the thick envelope of documents they'd been given by their father in New York. "Dad wants this delivered today."

Joe got up off the bed and took the envelope from Frank, hoisting it as if to test its weight and then holding it up to the light. "How do you figure this sting is going to work?"

"We're not getting involved in that part of it," Frank warned, taking the envelope back.

"Yeah, but let's just say how it might work," Joe persisted.

"The way I understood it, Appel is just the middleman for the real thieves," Frank said. "So if I were setting up a sting—"

"I'd trap Appel committing a criminal act," said Joe. "And when I had the goods on him—"

"You'd make a deal," Frank concluded. "He tells the authorities who has the gold, and in exchange he gets less of a jail term."

Joe nodded. "That's a sting, all right."

"And none of our business," Frank reminded him. "All we're supposed to do is deliver the documents."

"Right," Joe said, gazing out the window. "And then I intend to spend the rest of our Thanksgiving vacation having some fun."

They left the hotel room and found their way down to the street, where Joe immediately raised his hand to hail a cab.

"No cabs," Frank said. "If something goes wrong, I don't want Appel to be able to trace us through the driver back to the hotel. We go on foot."

"Don't you think you're being a little paranoid?" Joe asked, but he followed Frank through the narrow streets and even offered to navigate from a city map.

At a square called the Muntplein, the Hardys found themselves utterly confused. Half a dozen streets and a canal all seemed to come together at once. The canal was lined with flower shops overflowing with tulips. It was the height of Amsterdam's morning rush hour. Pedestrians, bicycles, and cars filled the intersection.

Joe heard a loud clanging behind him and jumped aside as an electric-powered streetcar swept past, its metal wheels grinding on the rails set in the street.

"Appel's place is this way," Joe said, glancing up from his map and pointing. "It's on a canal called the Keizersgracht—that means Emperor's Canal."

They crossed a bridge over a canal and continued until they came to the Keizersgracht. Here the seventeenth-century houses lining the canal were the size of mansions, but many had small brass plaques with company names beside the doors, indicating they were offices. Many were diamond and gold dealers.

Finally they found the old mansion that housed Appel's offices. Stone steps with a wrought-iron railing led up to an imposing door. Just as Frank and Joe mounted the steps, the door opened. A dark-haired young man in a black leather jacket rushed outside. For a second the stranger paused, his dark eyes locked on them. Then he averted his face and hurried off.

"Have you ever seen that guy before?" Frank asked his brother.

Joe shook his head. "Didn't look anything like the picture of Appel that Dad showed us."

The Hardys stepped inside the building and found themselves in a wide foyer with an immense brass chandelier overhead. On one side a small sign read Johannes Appel.

Joe knocked. Silently the door swung open. In the large, elegant room he saw a man sitting stiffly at an antique desk.

"Mr. Appel?" Joe began nervously, his eyes fixed on the window beyond. "We're from the New York investment house of—"

He got no response.

Great, Joe thought. He doesn't speak English,

and we're going to have to find a translator. Some undercover operation this is going to be.

Then Joe realized that Frank was elbowing him in the ribs. "What?" he demanded in a whisper.

"Look at him!" Frank ordered. "Really look at him."

This time Joe did look at the bullion dealer.

Johannes Appel was perfectly still, his eyes gazing dully into space and a silver letter opener piercing his heart.

Chapter
Four

THE NEXT MORNING Nancy woke in a four-poster bed draped in ivory brocade. Although George had telephoned Merissa's apartment before going to bed the night before, there had been no answer—only Merissa's answering machine cheerfully asking them to leave a message. The grand duchess had insisted they stay at the castle rather than return to an empty apartment.

Nancy sat up beneath the down comforter and took in her luxurious surroundings. Although morning sunlight filtered in through the diamond-paned windows, the air in the third-floor guest room was chilly. The fire that a servant had built the night before in the room's hearth had burned to embers. Nancy gazed at the thick Oriental carpet and the elegant oak dressing table and wardrobe. I could get used to this, she thought, rising from her bed.

She was about to put on the clothing she'd worn the day before when she saw her suitcase sitting just inside the door. That was odd, since she and George had left their luggage at Merissa's, expecting to go back there after dinner the night before. A note tucked beneath the handle explained: "I sent a servant for your things. I hope you do not mind. Andrei."

Nancy dressed quickly in a green turtleneck sweater, tan wool pants, and tan suede ankle boots. Then she brushed out her reddish blond hair and went down the hall to wash her face in the marble bathroom where she had taken a long, luxurious bath the night before.

After coming out of the bathroom, Nancy knocked on George's door first, which was just down the hall from her own room. There was no answer. Nancy looked inside to find the room empty. George was probably already at breakfast, Nancy decided. She went downstairs to the second floor and walked along the corridor until she reached a door that looked familiar from the night before. She peeked inside. It was the library, also empty. She went farther along the hallway until it wound around and opened into the second-floor dining room. George, Emma, and the grand duchess were already seated at the huge banquet table, having breakfast.

"Good morning," the grand duchess greeted Nancy warmly. "I trust you slept well."

"Very well, thanks," Nancy replied.

"That's only because the tourists aren't here," Emma said cheerfully. "Tomorrow at this time the halls will be ringing with voices wanting to know how much it costs to heat this place."

"Emma!" the grand duchess said.

"Well, they will," Emma insisted, unabashed. "The local historical society conducts a tour here one day a week," she explained to Nancy and George. "The proceeds help us meet expenses because the castle really is very expensive to maintain."

"Emma, please!" the grand duchess reproached her again. This time Emma pretended to be very busy buttering her toast.

Nancy was surprised to discover that the Romanov–von Badens would have to worry about money. Everything in the castle was lavish, and there were a number of servants waiting on its three residents, not to mention what Merissa had told George about Andrei—how he flew her to Paris for lunch and took her skiing in Switzerland. Nancy was sure that the price of his car alone could probably feed a family for a number of years.

Nancy looked at George. "Any word from Merissa yet?"

George shook her head. "I've been up for two hours. I keep calling the apartment, and there's no answer."

39

The grand duchess reached over and placed her hand on George's. "As Andrei's fiancée, Merissa has become very important to us."

"It's true," Emma said earnestly. "She's better than Andrei deserves, and Grandmama doesn't want her to get away."

The grand duchess gave her granddaughter another reproving look, then continued, "Everything will work out, George. You must not worry. Andrei will find her."

"Where is Andrei?" Nancy wondered.

"He left early this morning," Emma told her. "Andrei always has business in the city."

"What sort of business?" Nancy asked, curious.

The grand duchess smiled. "Investments. Andrei oversees certain funds that belong to the estate."

"If Andrei's in Amsterdam, then how will we get back to Merissa's apartment?" George asked.

"If Andrei does not return soon, we can send a car into the city," the grand duchess replied easily. "I do think, however, you should leave your things here until we know for certain that Merissa is back. As Merissa is soon to be part of our family, it is only right that we look after her friends. Now you must tell me what you are planning to do on your stay in the Netherlands. Of course, you'll want to see the works of the Dutch masters."

"Do you mean the painters?" George asked.

"The master painters of Holland," Emma said.

"Artists like Hals, de Hooch, van Ruisdael, Vermeer, and Rembrandt."

"You must have Andrei or Emma take you to the museums," the grand duchess went on. "You'll want to start with the Rijksmuseum."

Emma wrinkled her nose. "The museums are so stuffy. We'll take you to a place that's even better. You can see Jaap van der Meer's private collection."

"Who is Jaap van der Meer?" Nancy asked, noticing a brief flicker of something that might have been annoyance cross the grand duchess's face.

The doors to the dining room opened before Emma could answer, and Andrei strode in, his long coat open to reveal a black suit and a crisp white shirt.

"Jaap is an old family friend," Andrei answered. "Has Emma been telling you about his art collection? Merissa saw it a few weeks ago."

"Have you heard anything from her?" George asked anxiously.

"I'm sorry," Andrei said quietly.

George bit her lip. "I'd like to go back to Amsterdam and wait in her apartment."

"I'll take you myself," Andrei offered. "I'll be returning to the city shortly."

George stood up, a look of relief on her face. "Thank you for all your help," she said to the grand duchess.

The old woman rose from her chair. "No thanks are necessary," she replied graciously.

"Merissa will soon be a part of our family. Her friends are our friends."

She held her hand out to Nancy, and Nancy fought a strange urge to curtsy. The duchess was a small, frail-looking woman, and the top of her head barely came to Nancy's nose. Yet she radiated authority and old-world elegance. She's truly regal, Nancy thought in awe.

With breakfast over, Nancy and George started back to their rooms for coats and gloves.

"This place is so wild," George said as they rounded the corner to the long, wide corridor that stretched along the entire length of the castle's second floor. "If I knew Merissa was okay, I'd be having a great time."

"I know what you mean," Nancy said, stopping to look at a huge tapestry hanging on the wall. "When the grand duchess was talking about Merissa being family, I was thinking, it wouldn't be so bad becoming part of this family."

"I wonder if marrying Andrei will make Merissa a princess," George mused.

Nancy turned away from the tapestry and saw someone she hadn't expected at the end of the long hallway. She stopped and put a hand on George's arm. Just outside the doors that led to the library, the groundskeeper, Ot Schrijver, stood close to the wall, his back to the girls. He tapped a wood panel, then placed his ear against it, as if he expected to hear something. Nancy watched, fascinated.

What is he doing in this part of the castle? Nancy wondered. And what is he searching for?

"Wait here!" Frank ordered Joe, turning away from the corpse sitting at the desk. "And don't touch anything! I'm going after that guy we just passed on the way in here."

He raced out to the street and ran in the direction the man in the leather jacket had gone, almost colliding with several Amsterdammers who were passing on their bicycles. The man in the leather jacket was nowhere to be seen.

Frank spotted the blue uniform of a police officer. For a second he hesitated. The man had long brown hair down to his shoulders and wore a tiny gold earring in one ear, but the badge on his shoulder clearly read Policie, and he carried a walkie-talkie and a rubber truncheon.

Frank ran across the street to him. "Do you speak English? I need the police. My brother and I have found a body."

The policeman understood English perfectly. He spoke quickly into his walkie-talkie, then followed Frank back to the old mansion on the Keizersgracht.

Alone with the body in Johannes Appel's office, Joe examined the room, his eyes noting the expensive French furniture and immense gilt-framed mirrors on the walls. The desk was perfectly neat, holding a leather-bound ink blotter, a date book, and a small set of scales. A rectangular gold-colored nameplate on the desk bore the bullion dealer's name.

Joe looked at the body, his eyes following the lines of the man's limp limbs. The blood had not yet fully dried. The man had been murdered within the last hour—perhaps even minutes earlier. Then he noticed Appel's hand, which seemed to be reaching toward something. It was a fountain pen, lying on the floor a few inches from Appel's lifeless fingers.

Joe knelt and looked at it closely. The pen was made of gold, with thin, spiraling lines etched in an intricate pattern. Engraved in a polished space on the barrel was the letter *A*.

A for *Appel,* thought Joe. He glanced back to the neat desk. There was no sign that Appel had been writing when his attacker entered. Was the dead man grasping for his pen, hoping to use it to write the name of his murderer before he died? It was worth speculating about, because it would mean the dead man had known the identity of his murderer.

Footsteps sounded in the hallway beyond the tall double doors. Frank burst into the room, the uniformed policeman on his heels. Joe heard the sound of sirens growing louder and more shrill. The policeman took a quick look at the body and motioned toward the wall at the far side of the room. "Please. Stand there."

Slowly Frank and Joe backed up and stood at one end of the room, their backs against a gilt side table that held an immense bronze candelabrum. The sirens outside were deafening. The Hardys heard car doors slam on the street outside.

"Your passports, please!" the policeman demanded firmly, putting out his hand.

Frank handed his over and nodded at Joe, who reluctantly took his passport from his jacket pocket. He dropped it into the policeman's hand. Several men in suits burst into Appel's office, accompanied by more uniformed police officers. One glanced quickly at the body but strode toward the Hardys. He wore a light tan trench coat over a gray suit and a white shirt. His face was young, but his eyebrows and disheveled blond hair were streaked with gray. He took the passports and glanced at the two boys, comparing their faces to the photographs.

"'Frank Hardy' and 'Joseph Hardy,'" he read from the documents. He flipped a few more pages until he found their entry stamps. "You arrived at Schiphol this morning," he said, examining the border control stamp. Frank saw the detective's thick eyebrows flutter with genuine surprise.

"And already you have found a body. Not a very pleasant welcome to our city. I am Detective Kroon of the Amsterdam police. Would you explain to me how you came across this?"

"We're couriers for a New York investment house. We had to deliver this to Mr. Appel." Joe held up the large brown envelope. "A call to the trade attaché at the American consulate should straighten things out."

Detective Kroon took the sealed envelope and examined the label. "And why should I bother with the American consulate? A death in Amsterdam is a Dutch affair."

Joe steeled himself and pushed on. "I just don't think there's much point in you wasting your time thinking that we're suspects when we can so easily prove we're not."

Kroon looked at Joe a moment. He weighed the envelope in his hand, as if debating. Finally he handed the passports to a younger detective and gave him instructions in rapid Dutch. The man disappeared.

"I think I know who did it," Frank said. "Or at least what he looks like."

The Dutch detective gazed at him. "And who is that?"

Frank told Kroon about the man in the black leather jacket whom they had passed on the stairs outside and how they had found the body. By the time the Hardys finished, a coroner had arrived. He examined the body while police photographers took pictures of everything. Ambulance attendants waited in the hall, with a gurney and a black zippered bag, until the coroner was finished.

The young detective who had disappeared with their passports returned and spoke in Dutch. Detective Kroon glanced several times at the Hardys. Finally he turned to them.

"A Mr. Thomas at the consulate is aware that you're in Amsterdam and vouches for your character," he said quietly. Frank saw Kroon's eyes narrow very slightly. "However, I will ask you to remain in the Netherlands for several days, until the police investigation is complete. Where are you staying?" he asked, offering them their passports.

"At the Hotel Doelen," Frank said, taking the documents back.

"I suggest you continue to stay there until you hear from us." Kroon jerked his head toward the door. "You can go now. I have a mess to clean up."

The Hardys left the old mansion and returned to their hotel, walking along a cobblestoned street beside the canal.

"I could really use that nap now," Frank admitted. On impulse, he turned his head to look back the way they had come. His eyes met those of the man in the black leather jacket, not more than a block behind them. They were being followed.

Frank jabbed Joe with his elbow. "That's him!" he shouted, sprinting after him. The man did an about-face and took off, racing down the steps and onto a boat rental platform floating in the canal. Before an attendant could stop him, he untied a motorboat and jumped in.

Joe leapt over the side of the canal and landed with a thud on the floating dock, while Frank ran down the steps at full tilt. The motor of the stolen boat burst to life, and the boat moved out into the water.

"Let's get him!" Joe shouted, racing toward a second motorboat tied up on the rental platform. He saw the key dangling in the boat's ignition and released the rope holding the boat to the dock as he jumped in. The attendant, still stunned by the abrupt theft of the first motorboat, moved to stop Frank.

He was too late. Frank sprinted across the floating dock and leapt for the boat. He fell into the rear seat as the motor roared to life. Joe pushed the throttle open and steered the boat out into the canal. He gunned it, and it licked through the dirty brown water, the bow sending up wide furrows of waves.

Ahead of them, a series of three bridges arched across the canal, each visible through the half-circle openings beneath them. It was, Joe thought, like looking down the barrel of an immense telescope. Their quarry almost disappeared in the darkness beneath the second bridge.

Frank pushed himself up, trying to get his balance while old townhouses flashed past. He stood just as Joe steered under the first bridge. The dark stone ceiling came straight at Frank's head, low, wet and hard. He ducked and felt the underside of the bridge replace the airspace where his head had been.

Joe saw the other motorboat burst into daylight and race full speed toward the third bridge.

Other boats moved at a slower pace, and Joe steered around them as best he could.

"Greetings." Frank crept over the seat and dropped beside his brother just as they burst into daylight.

"He's under the third bridge," Joe said. He steered under the second bridge, keeping the motorboat on course and heading straight for the third. Another canal intersected the one they were on, forming a T. The escaping motorboat veered left and disappeared.

The Hardys' boat shot under the third bridge and headed for the arc of light at the other side. The wake of the escaping boat had furrowed the water, and the bow of the hull pounded into the waves. As they approached the opening into the next canal, Joe steered left, and the boat swept into daylight.

Suddenly the other motorboat was there. The man in the leather jacket had turned around and was waiting for them.

"I don't believe this!" Joe groaned and steered frantically to the left. But there wasn't time enough to change course.

The man in the leather jacket steered straight for their boat, deliberately forcing Frank and Joe into a head-on collision!

Chapter

Five

P ANICKED, JOE WRENCHED the steering wheel to the right. The motorboat tilted, the bow rising dangerously high into the air. A wall of dirty brown water swept over them. The other motorboat came within inches of the Hardys' boat.

Frank caught a glimpse of the man in the leather jacket, hunched over the wheel. He was young, with dark brown hair, blue eyes, and pale skin. He veered the boat in a tight turn and sped off under the bridge.

Joe fought with the steering wheel, yanking it in the other direction to avoid hitting the brick side of the canal. The motorboat whined shrilly as the propeller came out of the water.

"We're going over!" Joe shouted.

Frank felt the motorboat rising sideways in the

air, still sliding across the surface of the water. It began to flip over. He and Joe lost their balance and tumbled into the dirty, ice-cold water.

"You see? We are back in the city already," Andrei said to Nancy and George as he maneuvered the Porsche through the narrow streets that led to the older part of Amsterdam. "It only takes fifteen minutes."

"That's because you were driving like a maniac," Emma replied from the backseat of the C 2 coupe, where she sat next to Nancy. The grand duchess had suggested that Emma accompany Nancy and George back into Amsterdam in case they needed help finding their way around. Emma had readily agreed, and both Nancy and George were glad she was along.

Andrei zoomed into a parking space beside the canal that Merissa's building faced.

"I'm afraid I can only walk with you a short distance, and then I must be off," he said as they left the car. "I have an appointment I must keep. But I'll check back as soon as I can. In the meantime Emma will take care of you."

Following the canal, the four of them walked toward Merissa's building. The weather had not improved any since their arrival the day before. Nancy shivered and pulled the collar of her coat more tightly around her neck. It was hard to feel optimistic about finding Merissa when the day was so damp and cold and gray.

"What's going on over there?" Nancy asked, seeing a crowd gather by the side of the canal.

"Probably some sort of traffic accident on the water," Emma replied.

Nancy's natural curiosity drew her to the crowd. She peered around the shoulder of a tall man in a wool cap and saw a small motorboat on its side, rapidly filling with water. Two young men surfaced beside it, struggling to get out of the heavy woolen jackets that made swimming all but impossible.

Nancy's eyes widened as the dark-haired one shrugged off his jacket and, with a familiar look of annoyance, let it disappear into the filthy waters of the canal. He began swimming toward the bank with strong, even strokes, followed a few seconds later by his light-haired companion.

"George," Nancy said quietly, "am I imagining things or is that—"

"Frank and Joe Hardy," George finished in the same undertone of astonishment. "We run into them in the strangest places."

Nancy bit back a grin. "Well, this is definitely one of their more memorable appearances." She and the Hardys had teamed up all over the globe to solve cases together. Now she watched as Frank and Joe, sopping wet and covered with slime, crawled out of the water to be met by a stern-looking Dutch police officer.

"You know these people?" Andrei asked, a slight note of disapproval in his voice.

"They're friends of ours from the States," George replied.

Nancy pushed her way through the crowd in time to hear the police officer questioning the Hardys about another boat.

"He deliberately set us up for a head-on collision," Frank said.

The officer looked skeptical but made notes in a small black notebook. "Where is this man now?"

Joe's teeth were chattering. "He—he was gone by the time we surfaced. But he had brown hair and was wearing a worn black leather jacket."

"What about my boat?" demanded a red-faced man in heavily accented English. "They take it, and they sink it!"

"We'll have it towed from the canal, and then you can settle with these young men for the expenses," the officer said.

"Dad's going to love this," Frank muttered.

The police officer frowned at him. "The water in the canals is not meant for swimming. I suggest you and your brother go to a hospital emergency room for tetanus shots at once."

"Tetanus will never get me," Joe vowed through chattering teeth. "I'm going to die of cold first."

Another police officer, this one carrying two wool blankets, stepped forward and handed one to each of the boys.

"We'll be in touch," the first officer told them.

Joe wrapped himself in the blanket and gave the owner of the boat a forced smile. "Can't wait."

The crowd began to break up, and Nancy stepped forward. "Did you two have a good swim?" she asked, trying to keep a straight face.

Both Hardys stared for a moment, then Frank grinned and said, "Figures we'd meet you here, Drew."

"Are you guys all right?" George asked.

"Never been better," Joe assured her. "Aside from being cold, filthy, and looking like drowned rats, we're absolutely perfect."

"Nancy, are these really friends of yours?" Emma asked, coming toward them with Andrei following close behind her.

"Frank and Joe Hardy, meet Princess Emma Romanov–von Baden and her brother, Prince Andrei," Nancy said.

An expression of dismay crossed Joe's face as he saw the beautiful young princess. "Ace timing, Hardy," he muttered to himself. He held out a wet hand to Emma. "Pleased to meet you. We must be making a great first impression."

Emma gave him a dazzling smile. "You are unforgettable. But you should not be standing here freezing. You should be getting tetanus shots now. There is a hospital not too far from here," she went on. "Perhaps I'd better show you. Then I could take you to a shop to buy new jackets." She smiled. "I don't think you can wear blankets for your entire visit."

As Emma talked with Joe, Frank moved to Nancy's side. "Joe and I found a body this morning," he said so only she could hear. "We need to talk."

Nancy thought quickly. She and George were going to check out Merissa's apartment and do what they could to find Merissa. She had no idea how long that would take. "How about—" she began.

Andrei's voice overrode her own. "If you are friends of George and Nancy's, you must come out to the castle. After all, they are staying there with us. Why not tomorrow morning for the tour? You can stay for lunch, and we can get to know one another properly then. Please," he went on in a magnanimous voice. "I will send a car into Amsterdam to pick you up."

"Sounds good to me," Frank said.

Nancy almost laughed. Andrei had not only arranged their meeting, but he was also having it chauffeured.

"Let me write down your hotel and your room number," Andrei said, reaching into his pocket. He frowned, his hand searching the inside of his pocket. "Ah, here." He pulled out a felt-tip marker. "Tell me where to reach you, and I will give you the number at the castle."

When Andrei and the Hardys had finished exchanging information, Andrei turned to Nancy and George. With a deep, elegant bow he kissed each of them on the hand. "I will be in touch soon," he promised.

George watched him go, an expression of amazement on her face. "If only he wasn't such a crazy driver," she murmured.

The group split up then. Emma took the Hardys to the nearest hospital, and Nancy and George continued on to Merissa's apartment, where they once again rang the bell.

Again there was no answer.

"We should have asked Andrei for his key," George said.

"Maybe the landlady will let us in again," Nancy suggested. "Let's try her bell."

She did and a moment later Mevrouw Wouters poked her head out her window. "Hello," she called down. "Didn't Merissa come home yesterday?"

"That's what we were going to ask you," George called back.

"One moment. I will let you in." Mevrouw Wouters's head disappeared from the window, and seconds later the latch on the ground-floor door opened. Nancy and George followed the steep, narrow stairs to the second floor, where the landlady stood waiting for them.

"You have not heard from Merissa?" Mevrouw Wouters asked.

"We stayed in the country last night," George explained. "But we left the number, and Merissa never called us. And she hasn't answered her phone today."

"That's not unusual for your friend," the landlady said kindly, taking out the key to Merissa's apartment and leading them up the stairs. "The stories Merissa writes often keep her away. She has too much curiosity, that one. Always asking questions."

"About what?" Nancy asked.

"Everything," the older woman replied. "Let me see. Recently it was about windmills."

"That sounds kind of tame for Merissa," George said. "She specializes in investigative pieces."

Mevrouw Wouters shrugged. "Who knows what the article was? She asked me about the windmill codes."

"What codes?" Nancy asked, fascinated.

Mevrouw Wouters reached the fourth-floor landing and opened the door to Merissa's apartment. "Here in the Netherlands the position of the sails on a windmill has often been used as a kind of secret signal," she explained. "Sometimes it was just a wife telling her husband to come home from the fields. But when our country was occupied—centuries ago during the Hundred Years' War, and even more recently during the Nazi occupation of World War Two—the windmills were used to send messages that the invaders couldn't decipher."

"I wonder what kind of story Merissa was using that information for," Nancy said. Her eyes swept the inside of the apartment, taking a practiced inventory. Nothing seemed to have been touched since she and George had been there the day before.

"Did you notice Merissa having any visitors in the last week?" Nancy asked Mevrouw Wouters.

"No," the landlady replied. "But then, I am not always here."

"We appreciate your help," George said. "We'll let you know as soon as we hear from Merissa."

Nancy also said goodbye to the landlady, and then she and George were alone in the apartment.

"She hasn't been back," Nancy said.

"Doesn't look that way," George agreed. She walked into the bedroom and played the messages on Merissa's answering machine and heard only her own calls and one from Andrei.

"I have an idea," Nancy said. "Where is Merissa's appointment book? If she had an interview yesterday, we can check if she ever showed up for it."

The two girls searched through the desk drawers. There was no appointment book. "Maybe she carries it with her," George said.

"Maybe," Nancy said. She stood for a moment looking at the laptop computer. "It shouldn't be here," she said. "I mean, if Merissa *were* working on a story, wouldn't she have taken her laptop with her?"

"Unless she hadn't planned to be gone overnight," George said. "And she wouldn't have taken it if she was just doing an interview."

"Let's see what's here." Nancy sat down in front of the computer, booted it up, and quickly scanned the operations directory. "I think I can get into her programs," she said, punching in a sequence of commands.

Seconds later Nancy had a complete list of everything Merissa had on the computer. One by one she began to call up the files. "This doesn't make sense," she said when she'd gotten about three-quarters of the way through. "There isn't anything here connected to writing. Merissa has graphics programs, a few games, and something that detects computer viruses, but nothing to do with news stories."

George was looking more and more concerned. "That's impossible. She turns in at least one story a week."

"Well, she doesn't keep them on this computer," Nancy said.

"How about these?" George said, removing a box of floppy disks from one of the desk drawers.

Nancy checked all the disks. "Formatted but blank," she reported a few minutes later. "Whatever it is we're looking for, I don't think we'll find it on the computer. George, if Merissa was going to hide something, where would it be?"

George thought for a moment before answering. "This may sound crazy," she said, "but when Merissa and I were kids, we used to play a game called Hide the Button. Merissa *always* hid the button in the hem of the living room drapes."

Nancy grinned. "This may be the first lead we've had so far."

She and George went into the living room,

where Nancy looked doubtfully at the narrow hem on the lace curtains.

But George was already searching. "I can't believe it!" she exclaimed as she tugged at something in the bottom fold of the curtains. She smiled ruefully and shook her head. "Merissa, you haven't changed!"

"What is it?" Nancy asked.

George opened her palm, revealing a microcassette. "And I saw a tape player on the end table in her bedroom."

"Let's hope this tape fits the player," Nancy said. In the bedroom they found that the pocket-size machine was indeed made for microcassettes.

Nancy felt herself holding her breath as George inserted the cassette into the player and pressed the On switch. A young woman's voice began to speak.

"Story idea for article on Jaap van der Meer's art collection."

George switched off the tape player. "That's Merissa's voice," she said.

Nancy nodded. "Let's see why she hid this tape."

George switched the player on again, and Merissa's notes continued. "Van der Meer is a wealthy local collector, owning some of the most valuable paintings in Europe. Known and respected throughout art world. Van der Meer also lauded as a leader of the Dutch Resistance during the Second World War. So need further proof to support research from Central Library indicating his part in crime. If true, will scandalize Dutch society. Van der Meer was born in . . ."

Merissa went on for a while with basic biographical facts about Jaap van der Meer. Then a ringing bell interrupted her, and Merissa's voice stopped.

"The doorbell," George said.

The tape spun on with no sound except what might have been Merissa's footsteps across the hardwood floor. Suddenly Merissa's voice spoke again, this time her words coming out in a rush. "I don't believe it. He's sent his men. I have to get out of here!"

Nancy and George exchanged surprised glances. Merissa's last sentence was almost hysterical.

"I've got to hide this," the missing reporter said on the tape, "and find a way out!"

Chapter

Six

NANCY STARED AT the tape player. Merissa's frantic cry was followed by a click and then silence. "That click was Merissa shutting off the tape player," Nancy said.

"She must have hidden the tape right after that," George finished. "Before whoever was coming up the stairs found her." She looked up at Nancy, her face white with fear. "Nan, Merissa isn't out working on a story. Someone's kidnapped her!"

Nancy nodded slowly in agreement. "Isn't Jaap van der Meer the same man Emma wants us to see?"

"I think so," George said. "But we don't know for certain that whoever was at Merissa's door is connected to him."

"No," Nancy agreed. "I think it's time we called the police."

Nancy made the call and was connected with an English-speaking officer.

"Merissa Lang," he repeated the name. Nancy could hear him shuffling through papers. "Ah, yes, we had a similar report filed a short while ago by Prince Andrei Romanov–von Baden. He was very concerned, but unfortunately unless we have evidence that a crime has been committed, there is very little we can do to find her."

"We found a tape she hid in the apartment," Nancy told him. She described the mysterious message on the microcassette.

The policeman heard her out and then asked in a patient tone, "Are you trying to tell me that you think your friend was abducted and that Jaap van der Meer is involved?"

"It's possible," Nancy said.

There was long silence before the officer spoke again. "Ms. Drew, Jaap van der Meer is one of the Netherlands' most respected citizens and a decorated war hero."

Nancy sighed, knowing the detective didn't want to believe her. "We'd appreciate it if you listened to the tape."

"Very well," replied the clipped voice on the other end of the line. "Bring it in and I will listen to it. Thank you for calling."

Nancy put down the receiver and looked at George. "I have a feeling that phone call didn't do much good. Sorry."

George gazed around the apartment as if she hadn't even heard Nancy's last words. "Merissa recognized whoever rang her doorbell. She knew they were coming after her, and she was afraid."

"The police told me to bring the tape in," Nancy said.

"Don't," George said suddenly. "At least not until we make a copy. It's our only piece of real evidence that Merissa's been abducted. Besides, I think Andrei should hear it." She ran a hand through her short, dark hair. "Let's try the *Tribune* office," she suggested. "I'll make this call."

Nancy listened as George asked questions. She could tell that George wasn't getting any answers. "I could find out only what Andrei's told us," George reported at last. "Merissa was last in the office three days before we arrived. No one's seen or heard from her since, and no one is sure what she was working on."

A short time later the phone rang. It was Andrei. "Any word from Merissa?" he asked, sounding upset.

"None," Nancy answered.

Andrei sighed. "I've contacted the police. Unfortunately, they were not much help. I can't imagine where she would be."

"Neither can we," Nancy said. "But we found a tape she hid in the apartment. We think you should listen to it."

"Of course," Andrei said. "Why don't we listen to it back at the castle? I know that my grandmother will want to hear it. Actually, I just called to tell you I was returning home and ask if you two wanted a ride back. I also thought that we might stop first to have lunch at one of my favorite cafés."

Nancy hesitated a moment before answering. She and George could go find Frank and Joe, but George, who was standing by the window, was shaking uncontrollably. "That would be great," she told Andrei. "What about Emma?"

"She'll call the castle and have a car sent to pick her up when she's ready to go home," Andrei said easily. "Don't worry about my little sister. She manages quite well."

Nancy hung up the phone. "Are you okay?" she asked her friend.

"Fine," George said, not turning to look at her. "Who was on the phone?"

"That was Andrei," Nancy replied. "He didn't sound much better than you look. He's going to stop by and take us to lunch. Then we'll go back to the castle. I don't think there's anything more we can do here today."

George nodded. "Whatever."

An hour and a half later, when Nancy, George, and Andrei arrived back at the castle, Emma met them on the front steps.

"When did you get back?" her brother asked, removing a long silk scarf from his neck.

"About twenty minutes ago," Emma replied. "I had Grandmama send Pieter with a car. It was a much more civilized ride."

"Are Frank and Joe all right?" Nancy asked.

The princess smiled as they passed through the great front door. "The emergency room doctor gave them shots for tetanus, typhoid, and cholera," she reported. "So they were both very grouchy. But the doctor said they looked fine. I left them back at their hotel. They decided to rest, then go out and buy new jackets." Her blue eyes met George's dark ones. "Any sign of Merissa?"

"We found a tape hidden in her apartment," George replied. She was calmer than she'd been at Merissa's, but she still looked unusually pale.

"Grandmother will want to hear it," Andrei said.

"Then come into the library," Emma said, hooking an arm through George's elbow. "I'm sure my grandmother is in there."

The grand duchess turned to greet them as they entered the library. She was standing in front of the telescope again. *What does she see out there?* Nancy wondered.

"Grandmother," Andrei said, "Nancy and George found a tape that Merissa made."

"Have you listened to it?" the grand duchess asked.

"We'll play it for you," George offered, turning on Merissa's tape recorder.

The Romanov–von Badens listened to the tape in silence. Andrei was the first to speak. "We all knew Merissa was interested in doing a profile of Jaap. I took her to see his collection to help her with the story. But a crime connected with Jaap? That's preposterous! And I don't understand the end of the tape. Whose men is she talking about?"

Nancy knew she had to be diplomatic. "Is it possible that there is some hidden crime in Jaap van der Meer's past?"

"No," the grand duchess replied firmly. "I have known Jaap since before the war. He has nothing to hide. He is a man of tremendous courage and honor, whose deeds are a matter of public record." Her voice softened, and she took Nancy's hand. "Truly, child, even I have lost count of how many times he risked his life during the war, helping others whose lives were in peril."

"What about the men who were coming up the stairs at the end of the tape?" George asked.

"They couldn't be connected with Jaap," Andrei said. "George, you are talking about someone harming my fiancée. Jaap has always been like an uncle to me. He would no more harm my wife-to-be than he would harm Emma."

Before either Nancy or George could object, the grand duchess took the cassette out of the tape player and handed it to Andrei. "You must take this to the police at once," she told her grandson.

"Wait," Nancy said, more forcefully than she intended. "Actually, I was going to give it to the police but—"

"Forgive me, Nancy, but if *you* take it to the police, it will stay on someone's desk," the grand duchess said gently, her tone taking the sting out of the words. "But I'm sure they won't dismiss this if Andrei brings it to their attention."

"Grandmother is right," Andrei said with a disarming smile. "It really is the only thing my title is good for—getting attention. You might as well let me use it on Merissa's behalf."

"That would be great," Nancy said. "But we'd like to make a copy of it first."

"I will be happy to make a copy for you," the prince offered graciously.

At that moment a maid entered the library. She carried a small parcel, which she handed to the grand duchess. "It has just been delivered, ma'am," she said, curtsying slightly.

"Who is it from?" the elderly woman asked, examining the small brown box.

"I wouldn't know, ma'am," the maid said. "Mijnheer Schrijver said it was left at the gatehouse." She quickly left the room.

"Open it, Grandmother," Andrei said, handing her a silver letter opener from a nearby desk. "Perhaps it's a gift from a secret admirer," he teased.

The grand duchess slit the paper wrapping and opened the lid of the small cardboard box. She took out a mass of tissue paper and pulled it away. In the center of it was a small, blue porcelain monkey.

Nancy saw a strange look, almost one of shock, cross the old woman's face. Her hands trembled, and the blue monkey fell to the floor, shattering into dozens of pieces. The grand duchess clenched her hand to her chest over her heart. She'd gone pale and was fighting hard to catch her breath.

"Grandmama!" Emma cried. "Your heart."

Nancy stepped forward as the elderly woman sagged and helped her sit on the sofa behind her.

"My—my nitroglycerin!" the grand duchess gasped.

"Here it is, Grandmother." Andrei had pulled open a drawer in the antique desk. He took out a bottle of tablets, then ran to her side.

They all watched tensely as the grand duchess put one of the tablets under her tongue. Almost at once her breathing eased, and the pain left her face.

"Thank you," she said in a weak voice.

Nancy looked at the shattered statue on the floor. "It's too bad that it broke," she said. She knelt to pick up the pieces. "Maybe with some glue, we could—"

"Don't touch it," the grand duchess broke in sharply. "The maid will clean it up. I will not have my guests cut themselves over a piece of broken pottery. Andrei, be a dear and ring for the maid."

"Of course, Grandmother," Andrei said, tugging on a bellpull. He turned to Nancy and

George. "Have you seen the Romanov collection of Fabergé eggs? They are exquisite jeweled eggs that were created for Czar Nicholas's court before the Russian Revolution. Very few still exist. Come with me to the drawing room on the main floor, and let me show them to you."

Nancy and George let themselves be escorted out of the library and down to the first floor. But Nancy was troubled by the events of the last two days—Merissa's strange absence, a tape that seemed to point to Jaap van der Meer as her abductor, and now the odd incident with the blue monkey. They didn't really add up to much, she had to admit, but they led her to one conclusion: Something was being covered up in the Romanov–von Baden castle, and she intended to find out what it was.

Joe Hardy barely felt awake the next morning as he gazed at the castle's cobblestoned courtyard. Pieter, the Romanov–von Badens' chauffeur, had picked them up at the Hotel Doelen after breakfast, then deposited them at the front doors of the castle. Joe rubbed his hands together in the cold morning air and stared at the huge red-brick walls that rose in front of him.

"You know," he said to Frank, "somehow when Andrei invited us out here yesterday, I didn't really take the castle part seriously."

"I know what you mean," Frank said. "This place has a moat and a drawbridge and everything."

Seconds later a bus drove in through the wide gate and disgorged a load of tourists.

"I guess that's our tour," Joe said.

The two boys trailed the group into the castle. To Joe's relief, Nancy, George, and Emma were waiting for them in the great hall.

"We're going to take the tour with you," Nancy explained.

"Though I think Andrei's already shown us every square inch of this place," George added.

"Impossible," Emma told them. "Andrei is a very sloppy tour guide. He only shows you what interests him, which is mostly what Grandmama has told him he will inherit." She smiled at Joe. "I'm going to take the tour, too. Then we can all have lunch when it's over."

The historical society's tour guide led them through the numerous rooms on the first floor, showing the tourists the collection of enameled Fabergé eggs in the drawing room and a magnificent collection of medieval suits of armor in the room next to it. Afterward the guide led the group outside.

"The castle was originally built as a fortress in the thirteenth century," the guide explained. "It's been added on to ever since. Of course, the windows were enlarged when it was no longer needed as a fortress. But the castle's place in history has continued into this century, when it was used as a hiding place by Resistance fighters during the Second World War."

The guide stopped in front of a chipped brick

wall in the outer courtyard. "Do you see the bullet holes? This is where eight of those Resistance fighters were shot by the Nazis."

Frank shot Joe a look, which Joe had no trouble interpreting: Could the Resistance fighters who died here be the same ones connected to the stolen gold? It was impossible to tell without research—Resistance fighters had died all over Holland during the Second World War.

By the time the tour was almost over, Joe found himself paying less and less attention to the castle and more and more to Emma, who was wearing a blue sweater, the same shade as her eyes, and a white wool skirt.

Following Emma, Joe drifted happily to the back of the tour crowd. He jumped as he suddenly felt Frank's elbow jabbing him in the ribs.

"What is it?" Joe asked.

Frank nodded to the crowd ahead of them.

Joe followed his gaze. To his amazement, he saw that the mysterious man in the black leather jacket was among the tourists. The man was gazing straight at the Hardys, his eyes wide with disbelief.

Joe didn't stop to think. Without an explanation for Emma or anyone else, he set off after him. The man in the leather jacket broke from the crowd and tore across the cobblestoned courtyard toward the wide iron gates. Joe heard the sound of Frank's footsteps pounding behind him.

"Cut him off!" Frank shouted.

Yeah, sure, Joe thought. The guy seemed to be running a three-minute mile. Joe pushed himself harder, but the man in the leather jacket was widening the gap between them. He darted between the gates and across the wooden drawbridge, then over the bridge. A small black car was parked on the road, just beyond the bridge. The man jumped into the driver's seat and drove off.

Joe slid to a stop, panting. Something on the ground caught his eye. Was it something the man had dropped? Joe reached down and picked up a white matchbook. On it were the words *Club Paradiso*.

Twenty minutes later Frank, Joe, Nancy, and George met on one of the castle parapets, where they could speak in private.

"We'd better make this quick," Joe said. "I told Emma I'd be back downstairs in five minutes. She's answering questions from the tour group."

"What happened to the guy you two were chasing?" Nancy asked. "And who is he?"

"He's the man we saw just before we found our dead body yesterday," Frank answered.

"The same one who totaled our boat," Joe added. "He may be the murderer. And he got away again today."

Frank filled the girls in on their case. "I don't

know how the guy in the leather jacket connects to Johannes Appel," he concluded. "And I still can't believe that somehow he followed us out here."

"I don't think he did," Nancy said. "I was watching him. He looked every bit as surprised to see you as you were to see him."

"Are you saying his being here was a total coincidence?" Joe asked skeptically.

"Not exactly," Nancy replied. "He probably had a reason for being at the castle that had nothing to do with the tour. But I don't think you were that reason. There have been some pretty weird things going on here." She explained about Merissa's disappearance and the other mysterious events at the castle.

"What do we do next?" George asked glumly. "We've got two cases without any clues."

"Oh, we've got a clue," Joe said, holding up the matchbook. "I'd say our next move is to check out the Club Paradiso."

"Emma was telling us that a lot of the clubs in Amsterdam have afternoon concerts," Nancy said. "Why don't we check out the Paradiso tomorrow afternoon? But we'd better go back downstairs now. Lunch here is served at noon, and the grand duchess expects us all to appear."

"Would you please pass, uh, whatever's in that dish?" Joe asked Emma, who was seated next to him at the grand banquet table.

"This is a traditional Dutch food," Emma said, handing him the serving bowl. "It's made of spinach and sausage."

Nancy watched, amused, as Joe hesitated a moment, then made a valiant effort to look as though he was enjoying the dish.

"I have good news for all of you," Emma announced. "I have called Jaap van der Meer, and we are all invited to his townhouse this afternoon to see his private art collection."

"Emma!" the grand duchess said, a note of disapproval in her voice. "You know Jaap is a busy man. You shouldn't bother him."

"He didn't mind," Emma replied. "He said he wanted to meet my American friends."

The doors to the dining room opened, and Andrei walked in, a newspaper in hand. He looked distraught. "I'm sorry I am late," he said, "but I cannot believe this!" He pointed to the article on the front page of the newspaper and translated the opening sentence. " 'Johannes Appel, a gold dealer, was found murdered in his Keizersgracht office. . . .' "

Appel, Nancy thought, looking across the table and meeting Joe's knowing eyes. "Did you know him?" she asked Andrei.

"He did some work for the family," the prince replied in a distracted way.

Nancy stole a quick look at Frank, at the other end of the table. He was gazing at her and, it seemed to Nancy, undoubtedly thinking exactly the same thing: Maybe there was a connection between their cases.

Suddenly a shiver crept up her spine. If the young man in the leather jacket really is the murderer of the bullion dealer, Nancy thought, is he now stalking the Romanov–von Badens?

Chapter

Seven

ON THE RIDE into Amsterdam in the Romanov–von Badens' black limousine, Joe had felt a familiar tension among the four Americans. All of them knew that somehow Jaap van der Meer was important to solving the mystery of Merissa's disappearance. But as none of them were sure of what they'd find inside his townhouse, they had no formal plan. They'd have to observe carefully and glean what information they could. As far as Joe was concerned, there was only one distraction—Emma Romanov–von Baden.

The young princess ordered Pieter, the chauffeur, to let them out in Dam Square, in front of the Royal Palace. It was a grand old building of gray stone almost as big as a city block. On one side a slender Gothic cathedral rose above the roofs of four-hundred-year-old houses.

"Jaap's townhouse is on the Singel, a canal that's only a block away," Emma explained to her new friends. "I thought you'd like to walk from here."

"Do you want me to wait for you, miss?" Pieter asked her before stepping back into the limousine.

"No, that's all right. I'll call when we're ready to go back," Emma told him. She caught Joe's glance and turned to him, curious. "What are you smiling at?"

"You," he replied, "and that cool, polite tone. You're what—sixteen? And you've probably been ordering servants about since the day you were born."

Emma blushed. "It isn't quite like that. They do as I ask out of loyalty to my family. And I try to ask only for what is necessary."

"I see." Joe was finding himself thoroughly intrigued by the young princess. He'd had plenty of girlfriends, but he'd never gone out with a princess. He was beginning to wonder if it was even possible. He tried to imagine Emma visiting his totally average house in Bayport.

They crossed Dam Square, which was filled with pedestrians and street musicians. Shoppers streamed from the nearby Kalverstraat, and teenagers loitered around the war memorial opposite the palace. Cars, bicycles, and long, noisy streetcars swerved at rapid speed around the wide cobblestoned square.

Emma led them around the palace so they could see the cathedral. They crossed a busy street, then a bridge over the canal.

"The Singel is one of Amsterdam's most exclusive places to live," Emma told them when they reached the other side. Huge old townhouses, some made of brick, others of gray stone, lined the canal.

"What are they doing?" Nancy asked, pointing to a nearby house on the corner of a side street. There was an enormous stuffed sofa on the sidewalk, and workers were tying ropes around it.

"Someone's moving furniture into the house," Emma explained. She pointed to the gables of the brick house, five stories overhead. A beam jutting from the gable held a pulley, and a long, thick rope was doubled through it. The glass had been removed from the fourth-floor window, and another worker stood in the opening.

"See that heavy beam sticking out from the roof just beneath the gable? And the rope hanging from it? They will use it to lift the sofa up through that fourth-floor window. In Holland the staircases are too narrow to move furniture, so this is how we do it."

The four friends watched the workers tie the rope from the pulley to the sofa. A moment later they began to pull. The rope slid through the pulley, and the sofa floated high into the air. When it was opposite the fourth-floor window, the sofa was pulled inside and untied. Then the mover dropped the end of the rope down to the ground.

The four Americans watched with astonishment as a dining table, a bookcase, and a large desk followed the sofa through the window.

"Amazing," Frank muttered.

"It's done all the time," Emma assured him. "Even pianos go through the windows in Amsterdam." She glanced at the delicate gold watch on her wrist. "Jaap's house is just around the corner, and he'll be waiting for us."

A few moments later Joe gazed up at the imposing gray stone townhouse that belonged to Jaap van der Meer. Like most houses in Amsterdam, it was five stories high and connected on either side to other houses. But the van der Meer townhouse was one of the most elegant houses Joe had seen, nearly three times as wide as most others.

Carved stone lions, eagles, and mermaids edged its windows and gables. An oval stone set above the door indicated that the house had been built in the early seventeenth century. Heavy curtains covered the windows, which to Joe seemed odd in a city where most of the curtains were open.

Emma walked up the short flight of steps to the front door and rang the bell. Moments later an elderly butler wearing a black day coat opened the door. With a short bow, he admitted them to the townhouse.

Joe wasn't sure what he'd expected van der Meer to look like, but he wasn't prepared for the slender, elegant man with thick, snow white hair brushed back from a strong hawklike face.

"Emma!" Jaap van der Meer said, taking her hands in his. "I'm so glad you came to visit. You must introduce me to your new friends."

"This is Frank and Joe Hardy," Emma began. "And this is George Fayne and Nancy Drew. George is a good friend of Merissa's."

"How is Merissa?" Jaap van der Meer inquired. "I have not seen her since Andrei brought her by a few weeks ago."

"She seems to have disappeared," George said quietly. "We came to Amsterdam two days ago to visit her, and she still hasn't shown up."

Van der Meer raised one snowy eyebrow. "That is most disturbing. But she is a journalist, is she not? Perhaps she has gone on an assignment somewhere."

George shrugged. "She certainly didn't leave any messages with anyone."

Van der Meer looked taken aback. "Have you spoken with the police?"

"Yes, and so has Andrei," Emma answered.

"I will put in a word myself," Jaap promised. "You never know what will make them move more quickly. Now, as you are here to see my art collection, allow me to do the honors."

They were standing in the front hallway, although it was not just any front hallway. Elaborate gilt-covered plasterwork divided the walls into panels that drew the eye upward to a vaulted ceiling painted with a mural of fierce-looking angels. A heavy crystal chandelier dropped from the center of the dome, throwing bits of reflected light onto the walls. At the end of the hall a polished, dark wood staircase went up to the second floor.

"The style is called rococo," van der Meer said, following Joe's gaze. "It's a bit ornate, but to my taste. Come, you must see the work of the true masters."

He led them farther into the house. George stopped to admire a graceful wooden chair upholstered in silk brocade. "Louis Seize," their host said casually.

"Louis says what?" Joe asked.

"Louis the Sixteenth." Nancy laughed and translated the French. "He was a French king. That style of chair was popular during his reign."

"I beg your pardon," van der Meer said graciously. "That chair is an original from his court."

Of course, Joe thought, trying hard not to dislike his host.

The man stopped in front of an oil painting of a middle-aged woman wearing a wide-brimmed hat. The painting was really not Joe's taste. His own walls at home were covered with football posters, but even he had to admit that there was something extraordinary in the portrait. The woman stood against a dark wall. The very edge of the wall had a soft, golden glow to it, as if it were catching the last rays of the afternoon sun. The woman herself seemed real. Joe had the uneasy impression that at any moment she might turn her head and begin to speak. The artist had taken a flat image and breathed life into it.

"Rembrandt van Rijn," van der Meer said quietly. "He is often called the Lord of Light."

Next he led them to a portrait of a man examining a globe. Again, Joe had the sensation that if he touched the man's sleeve, he'd find a living person inside it.

"Vermeer," their host informed them. "A very rare work. One of only forty-seven paintings that bear his signature."

The tour continued through the first three floors of the townhouse. Joe's head began to spin with the names of artists: Bosch, Brueghel, van Eyck, van Ruisdael, de Hooch, Steen, Maes, and even van Gogh.

"The guy who cut off his ear, right?" Joe asked.

Van der Meer gave him a look of mild disgust and said, "Quite so."

Finally the Dutch art collector led the group back to the main floor. "Our country is most fortunate to have such a magnificent artistic legacy."

Joe decided that since Jaap van der Meer was already convinced he had no manners, he might as well ask the question he was most curious about. "How much is all this stuff worth?"

The art collector's eyes widened briefly, and then he gave a diplomatically evasive answer. "You must understand, art of this caliber is priceless."

Emma giggled. "It's worth a fortune, Joe. Museums all over the world borrow pieces from Jaap's collection."

That was pretty much what Joe had figured. He had one more tactless question. "How does someone make enough money to afford art like this?"

Van der Meer smiled. "I had an inheritance, of course. And now I make my money from investments in Indonesia, which used to be a part of the empire."

"The empire?" Joe echoed.

"The Dutch Empire," van der Meer said in an arrogant tone. "Surely you Americans are taught *some* history."

Frank let out a long breath. "Not enough, I guess." He nodded toward a glass case filled with medals. "They look pretty historic."

"They were awarded to me for my work during the German Occupation," Jaap said.

George pointed to a large gold cross. "What do the words on this medal mean?"

"That's the motto Queen Wilhelmina bestowed on the city of Amsterdam for its Resistance efforts during the war," Emma answered. "It means 'Heroic, Resolute, Merciful.' When Jaap got that medal, she said he embodied all of those qualities."

"Emma, please!" van der Meer protested. "You'll embarrass me."

"It doesn't sound as if you have anything to be embarrassed about," Nancy said. "What sort of Resistance work did you do?"

"The Germans occupied Amsterdam for five years," Emma answered. "Jaap set up hiding places for the *onderduikers.*" She smiled at Joe. "That means 'divers.' It was our term for people who had to spend the war in hiding—Jews, Gypsies, homosexuals, Resistance workers— there were so many."

"What Emma is saying is true," van der Meer added. "By the summer of 1944 the cellars, attics, and secret rooms of this city hid almost as many people as the Germans had transported to the Third Reich for forced labor."

"Jaap also stole arms for the Resistance," Emma went on proudly. "And he forged documents to fool the Nazis."

"Enough!" the white-haired man said. "There is nothing worse than boring your guests with old war stories." They had reached the ornate front hallway again. "I believe," he said with good humor, "that concludes your tour of the van der Meer museum."

"But you haven't shown us the chalice!" Emma cried, disappointment in her voice.

"Oh, Emma, it is only an old cup."

"It's made of pure gold and set with rubies, sapphires, and emeralds, and it dates back to the twelfth century," Emma reminded him.

Van der Meer shrugged helplessly and looked at the Americans. "Would you like to see the chalice? It's in the study."

"Definitely," Joe said. He wasn't really all that keen on seeing an old cup, but the study was one room they hadn't been in, and he wanted to see as much of the townhouse as he could. Somewhere there had to be a clue to Jaap van der Meer's secret.

Jaap led them back to the second floor and down a narrow corridor. Joe guessed that the study faced the street and the canal, but it was impossible to tell. Heavy damask drapes covered the two tall windows, making the room seem dark despite its lamps.

Maybe because the room was dark Joe didn't see them at first. Two powerfully built men wearing dark suits sat in armchairs in a corner of the room. One was short and stocky; the other one was taller and thin. At a brief nod from Jaap, they left the room. Bodyguards, Joe thought instantly. They have to be bodyguards.

He was about to nudge Frank when he realized his brother was looking at a letterhead in a pile of mail on the desk. Joe's eyes widened as he recognized the name of the murdered gold dealer.

"Ah," van der Meer said, noticing Frank's curiosity. "You recognize the name from the headlines. Murdered yesterday. Terrible tragedy." He touched a light switch. A glass display case lit up, revealing the ancient jeweled chalice.

Nancy, George, and Emma gathered round to admire it, and Jaap began to tell them of its complicated history. Frank came close to Joe and whispered quietly, "Another connection to Appel."

When they had finished examining the jeweled chalice, van der Meer led them back downstairs. "It was a pleasure to meet all of you," he told them. "I hope you will enjoy the rest of your stay in our country."

"We will if Merissa turns up," George said, her tone curt. She had formed an instant dislike for the man. All she could think about were Merissa's words on the tape: ". . . his part in crime. . . . will scandalize Dutch society. . . ."

"Of course," van der Meer said. "As a friend of the Romanov–von Badens, I will do everything in my power to help you find her. After all, it would not do to have Andrei's fiancée disappear."

"Oh!" George said in a startled voice. She knelt and ran her hand through the deep pile carpeting.

"What is it?" van der Meer asked with concern.

"My contact lens popped out," George said.

"Let me help you look," Nancy said, kneeling beside her.

What's going on? Joe wondered. He was willing to bet that George had never worn a contact lens in her life.

"Got it," George said, standing up and making

a production of taking a tissue from her shoulder bag and wrapping it around the imaginary lens. "I'll have to soak it when we get back to the castle."

Joe threw a questioning glance at Nancy, who mouthed the word "later" in answer.

Once outside Jaap van der Meer's house Nancy turned questioningly to George. Emma was walking ahead of them between Frank and Joe. "What was that contact lens business all about?" she asked George.

George held out a tiny gold earring in the shape of a ram's head. "It's Merissa's. I saw it snagged in Jaap van der Meer's carpeting."

"Are you sure it's hers?" Nancy asked.

"Positive," George replied. "It's from the pair I gave her on her birthday last year. The ram is her birth sign, Aries. Nan, I don't trust Jaap. I didn't trust him from the minute I met him. I'm sure he knows where she is, and this earring proves it!" Her voice was getting louder, and she was speaking rapidly.

"Slow down a minute," Nancy cautioned. "Merissa has been to his house with Andrei. She could have dropped the earring then."

"No," George insisted. "If he last saw her several weeks ago, as he said, that earring would have been vacuumed up long ago. Merissa had to have been there recently. Besides," she went on, "van der Meer was just too smooth, too calm when I told him about Merissa being missing. He has something to do with her disappearance—I *know* it!"

Nancy looked at her friend with concern. "You may be right," she said. "I didn't like van der Meer, either. But we'll need more proof than that earring before we can accuse him of anything."

Emma and the Hardys were waiting at the corner. George gazed up the front of Jaap's townhouse, giving it a last, long, lingering look.

"Come on, George. Frank and Joe are waiting for us," Nancy prodded.

Suddenly George's face went pale. She pointed to the top of Jaap's townhouse, where there was a tiny circular window.

"Nancy!" she said, her voice a hoarse whisper. "Merissa's up there! I just saw her face in the window!"

Chapter

Eight

NANCY PEERED UP at the garret window but saw only dark, dusty glass. "Are you *sure* you saw Merissa up there?" she asked George doubtfully.

"Positive."

Frank Hardy walked back toward them, trailed by Joe and Emma. "What's going on?"

Nancy nodded toward the top of the townhouse. "George says she saw Merissa's face at the top window. Did any of you see anything?"

Joe looked puzzled. "Not me."

"Or me," Frank said.

"George, you can't really think Jaap had anything to do with Merissa's disappearance," Emma said. "Jaap is a family friend. He would never do anything to hurt someone."

"He stole guns and forged papers for the

Resistance," George reminded her in a cold voice. "He'd probably make a pretty good criminal if he put his mind to it."

Emma's face went white with anger. "I will pretend that you never said that. While you are a guest of my family, I must ask you not to repeat such an accusation."

"Merissa is missing," George said distinctly. "And if you can't understand—"

"I know you're upset," Emma broke in quickly. "But we'll find her. There's a public telephone at the corner. Why don't we ring her apartment again?"

Frank, Joe, and Nancy waited across the street while George and Emma went into the bright green telephone booth.

"George isn't in good shape," Frank observed.

"I know it," Nancy said, "and I don't blame her. I want to find Merissa as much as she does, but I don't think she's acting rationally. And if she keeps challenging people, she's going to make things worse." Nancy gave a deep sigh. "I feel as if I'm on my own on the case."

"You're not on your own," Frank said gently. "You've got us."

"Right," Joe agreed. "Here we are in Amsterdam with orders from Dad not to do anything on our case, so we might as well work on yours."

"Look," Frank said, "didn't you tell us that Merissa's tape mentioned finding data on van der Meer's past in the Central Library? She could have really been onto something. Maybe Joe and

I should do a little library research and see if we can dig up that same information."

Nancy smiled. "Thanks. That would be great. Especially since the grand duchess seems to be organizing most of our time. It's almost as if she's trying to distract us from something, but I don't know what. At least while you're at the library, maybe I can figure out what's really going on at that castle."

"Uh—" Joe sounded hesitant. "Would you mind if Emma didn't go back to the castle with you right now?"

Frank rolled his eyes. "Romeo strikes again."

"Give me a break!" Joe said. "Emma was upset by George accusing van der Meer. I want to talk to her about him."

"That might not be a bad idea," Nancy said thoughtfully. "I'd like to get as much information on that man as possible. I'll tell you what— George and I have been wanting to pick up some delftware for souvenirs. Why don't we meet you in an hour on the front steps of the palace in Dam Square?" She turned to Frank, her eyes twinkling mischievously. "Do you want to come shopping?"

"Uh—no thanks," Frank said. "I think I'll pass. I could use some time back at the hotel."

"See you in an hour," Joe said.

Emma led Joe to a quiet café on Rembrandtsplein, a square in the old part of the city surrounded by huge old hotels. The café looked out over the square, where birds gathered on an impressive bronze statue of the painter Rembrandt seated in a thronelike chair.

Joe and Emma sat at a table by the window and peered out from between red-checkered curtains at the people strolling through the square. Inside the café the scent of fresh-baked pastries filled the air.

"Do you have places like this in America?" Emma asked curiously.

"Sort of," Joe replied. "I mean, we have coffee shops and we have cities, but none of them feel like this. And in our country most of our statues are of war heroes, not artists."

Emma smiled. "We have some of those, too." She looked down at the menu. "You must try the *apfelgebaak,*" she said. "It is apple cake and a specialty of this café."

They ordered the apple cake and cups of hot cocoa spiced with vanilla. Joe waited until the waiter had left before saying, "I'm sorry for what George said to you outside Jaap's house."

Emma stared down at the red and white tablecloth, her long blond hair gleaming. "It was nothing," she said quietly. "I know George has been very worried about Merissa."

"She was pretty upset today," Joe agreed. "When we came out of the townhouse, she thought she saw Merissa's face in the attic window."

"That's impossible!" Emma said heatedly.

"Are you sure?" Joe asked.

"I've known Jaap since I was born," Emma replied. "He was at my christening."

The waiter brought their food, and Joe took a bite of the delicious apple cake, wondering how to continue the discussion. He liked the young princess and didn't want to offend her. "Jaap seems a little eccentric to me," he said at last.

Emma laughed. "He's extremely eccentric. He's always been a very secretive man. I think that's a habit left over from all his years in the Resistance."

"Or maybe he has something to hide," Joe said cautiously.

Emma's blue eyes looked at him curiously. "Actually, that's something I've always felt. I can't imagine what it would be, though." She smiled again, and Joe found himself wishing he weren't investigating her family friend.

"We all have our little secrets," Emma went on. "Tell me, Joe Hardy, what are yours?"

Joe stared at her in alarm. Did she suspect him of investigating van der Meer? Did she know that he and Frank were working undercover?

"I'll tell you mine," Emma offered. "I am to marry a prince who lives in Luxembourg."

Joe choked on his cocoa. "You what?"

"He is twenty-five and looks like a ferret—he has a very narrow face," the princess explained. "And I think that before I have to marry him, I will run away."

Joe reached out and took her hand. "Well, if

you do run away, why don't you consider running
to America?"

"And what would I do there?" Emma teased.

Joe couldn't help himself. He drew her close
and gently kissed her. "I don't know," he murmured. "But if you come to Bayport, I'm sure
we'll think of something."

Only minutes after Nancy and George reached
the palace, Joe and Emma showed up. Both of
them were smiling. Nancy was sure Joe had a
crush on the young princess.

"Did you find your delftware?" Emma asked.

Nancy held up a large shopping bag. "Souvenirs for everyone," she said. "Plus George and I
grabbed a quick snack."

"I'll call Pieter to come get us," Emma offered.

Nearly an hour later Nancy, George, and
Emma returned to the Romanov–von Baden
estate.

"Maybe Grandmama has heard something
about Merissa," Emma said as they entered the
castle.

They found the grand duchess in the library,
again staring through the antique telescope. This
time, Nancy noticed, the elderly woman moved
quickly away from the eyepiece as they entered
the library, as if she didn't want to be caught
looking through it.

"I'm glad you're back," the grand duchess said
to the girls. Although she was smiling, she looked
uneasy.

"Has there been any word on Merissa?" George asked tensely.

"None," the older woman said in a regretful voice. "I believe Andrei took the tape to the police sometime today, but so far we haven't heard from them."

Nancy signaled to George—an old hand signal they used when Nancy needed a distraction. For a second she wondered if George would respond. To Nancy's relief, George nodded almost imperceptibly, then pointed to an oil painting at the other end of the room and began asking Emma and the grand duchess questions about it.

Nancy waited until she was sure that neither the grand duchess nor Emma was looking in her direction. Quietly she moved to the telescope. Careful not to alter its position, she quickly peered through the eyepiece. Across a stretch of long, flat fields divided by grass-covered dikes, Nancy saw the four spidery sails of an old windmill in perfect focus.

Why would the grand duchess be staring at a windmill? Nancy wondered, moving away from the telescope. A memory nudged her, and she recalled Mevrouw Wouters's comments that Merissa had been asking questions about windmills. What was it the landlady had said? The sails were used to send secret signals during wars. Was someone using this windmill to send the grand duchess a message?

"Nancy," the grand duchess called. "Don't stand over there by yourself. Come talk with us."

Nancy yawned. "Would it be all right if I went upstairs for a while and took a nap? I think jet lag finally caught up with me."

"I know exactly how you feel," George said, also yawning. "I almost fell asleep in the car on the way back from the city."

"Then you must both rest at once," the grand duchess said decisively.

Nancy and George each went up to their rooms. Three minutes later George knocked on Nancy's door.

"What did you see through the telescope?" George asked as Nancy let her in.

Nancy walked over to the bedroom window. "Here, I'll show you. I just realized that this room is directly over the library, with the same view."

George gazed out the mullioned window. "All I see are fields and canals. I can't believe how many canals there are in this country."

"It's that windmill," Nancy told her, pointing toward the gaunt, towerlike shape in the distance. "I don't know why the grand duchess keeps staring at it, but I'm going to find out. Maybe it has some connection to those windmill codes Merissa was interested in. Want to take a walk?"

George seemed more like herself as she said, "Sure! I didn't really want to take a nap, anyway."

"The trick will be getting out of the castle without anyone seeing us," Nancy said.

"Especially the grand duchess," George

agreed. "If she finds out we're not sleeping, she'll plan some activity for us." George's voice rose in pitch as she mimicked the duchess's aristocratic tones: "You simply *must* let Emma show you every square inch of the castle. Twice."

Nancy laughed. "Exactly. We're going to have to stay out of view of that telescope. Remember we saw a back door on one of the tours?"

George's eyes lit up. "Of course! It's down by the kitchens, and it leads to a footbridge that crosses the moat."

They took a servants' staircase that spiraled down one of the castle's round corner towers to a corridor near the kitchens. An iron door was set in the stone wall, locked with two sliding metal bolts. Quietly Nancy slid them open.

She studied the bridge carefully. "This bridge doesn't look very old."

"No," George agreed. "Emma told me it was added only about a hundred years ago, long after the castle stopped being a fortress."

"I wonder if it ever has stopped being a fortress," Nancy mused as they crossed the bridge. "I mean, it almost feels as if there's a secret behind those walls—something the castle still guards, something that people would die to defend."

George gave a little shiver. "I hope not."

When they had crossed the footbridge, Nancy found a pebbled lane that led past the forest surrounding the castle and toward the windmill.

Nancy nodded, and they set off across the lane. There was no way to conceal themselves on the open landscape, but they were approaching the windmill from the side. They hoped they'd stay out of the duchess's line of view.

When they were a good distance from the castle, Nancy turned and looked back. She saw the square brick castle with its circular towers on each corner from a completely different angle and noticed something unusual. There was a fifth tower—windowless—that protruded from one wall.

"George, which rooms are in that windowless tower?"

George turned around and looked back at the castle. "The music room?" she guessed. "No, that faces the side of the castle."

Nancy frowned. "From the inside, I can't remember seeing a tower there at all, let alone the rooms in it. And we certainly didn't see any rooms without windows."

"You're right," George agreed, staring back at the castle with a puzzled expression.

"Considering that we've had thorough tours from Andrei, Emma, and the local historical society, I can't believe we skipped an entire tower," Nancy said. "Maybe it's closed up."

They continued walking toward the windmill. "Nan," George said, "I was kidding before when we were up in your room, but the grand duchess is starting to make me nervous. She organizes every minute of our time—this is practically the first time since we came to Holland that we've been alone together. She always seems to have either Andrei or Emma escorting us somewhere."

"I've noticed," Nancy said grimly. "She's controlling us and has been from the day we arrived. She was the one who had Andrei whisk us away to the castle, and I'll bet she's the one who sent for our bags."

"Sounds as if we're being watched," George said quietly. "Why is it so important that the Grand Duchess Anna Sergey-whatchamacallit keep an eye on us?"

"I don't know," Nancy admitted. "And I'm not sure what to do about it. I mean, part of me would love to leave the castle and the entire Romanov–von Baden clan. But there's something mysterious going on here, George. I'm sure it's connected to Merissa's disappearance." She gave her friend a rueful smile. "And you know me—I'm not very good at walking away from a mystery."

"Well, I'm not, either," George said, "and I still say I saw Merissa in that attic window."

Nancy gave her friend a hug. "George, you may be right. But it was a fifth-floor window, and a grimy one at that. Maybe you saw something—or someone—else. We've got to have more proof before we accuse someone—especially one of Holland's most respected citizens."

George let out a deep sigh. "Well, all I can say

is that we'd better come up with something soon."

They had almost reached the windmill. Even with a light breeze blowing across the fields, the long sails of the windmill rotated lazily.

Nancy gazed up at them. "Do you think someone's been leaving signals for the grand duchess?"

"Maybe there's something valuable inside it," George suggested.

To Nancy's surprise the door in the base of the building was unlocked. Cautiously she pushed it open. The inside of the mill was dark, and it took a moment for her eyes to adjust. She could just make out an assortment of tools hanging from the walls, things that looked as if they were used to maintain the windmill. In the center of the room a winding staircase led to a loft.

Nancy found a flashlight by the door and turned it on. Slowly she began to ascend the stairs. The old wooden staircase shook beneath her feet. She shone the light above her. "I don't see anything suspicious here," she told George, a note of disappointment in her voice.

"Neither do I," George said. "Whatever reason the grand duchess has for being obsessed with this place, I don't think it's because of the contents."

"Unless there's something hidden here," Nancy said. "But I'm not ready to tear apart the walls until we have an idea of who frequents this place and when."

Nancy made her way back down the stairs and twisted the knob on the outside door. "That's strange," she said. "It seems to be stuck."

"Let me try." George twisted and pulled at the knob and even kicked at the door before coming to the same conclusion Nancy had already reached. "We're trapped," she said. "Someone's locked us in!"

Chapter

Nine

Iт was nearly dinnertime when Frank and Joe climbed the stairs to the Central Library. They had just had an awkward long-distance conversation with their father. He had told them his insurance would cover the damaged motorboat. He had also pointed out that this wasn't one of their more cost-efficient operations.

"You think Dad was mad about the boat?" Joe asked as they entered the library's main room. It was a modern, utilitarian building, with long tables laid out among the stacks of bookshelves.

Frank winced. "Let's just say I've heard him sound happier." He glanced around the busy room. It appeared to be full of students. "We lucked out with the library being open till nine tonight. Let's just hope our luck holds and we can find someone who will translate Dutch to English."

Translation, Frank soon found out, wasn't necessary. Many of the books and magazines in the library were in English. As a librarian explained to them, "Of course we have references in English. It's the second language for most Dutch people."

Frank and Joe carried a stack of books and bound periodicals to an unoccupied table. They had one thing in common—all of them mentioned Jaap van der Meer.

Forty minutes later Joe looked up and crossed his eyes. "This stuff is all about van der Meer as a war hero, Resistance fighter, and all-around superman. I mean, you'd think he'd defeated the Nazis single-handedly."

"That's what most of this is, too," Frank said, gesturing to his own pile of sources. "He was pretty remarkable, though. He kept risking his life in these impossible situations, and he always seemed to pull it off. It's almost as if he had no fear."

"I'd better keep reading," Joe muttered. "I can't wait to find out how he saved the world from total evil."

Frank threw a pencil at his brother, and they both went back to the books. Frank was actually skimming the last of the books he'd borrowed from the stacks when something caught his interest.

"Joe, listen to this."

"Not if it's another tribute to Jaap of the Resistance," Joe said. "I'm sorry. I just can't take any more."

"Listen, anyway," Frank instructed. "It starts out with the Resistance stuff, but then it talks about gold bullion."

"As in the stolen gold we're investigating?"

"You got it," Frank said, grinning. "According to this account, during the chaos at the end of the war, the Nazis stole the gold from the Dutch bank and were about to ship it to Germany by railroad when the Resistance found out. A group of Resistance fighters disguised themselves as Nazi soldiers and 'rerouted' the gold onto trucks. Then they drove it to a safe place. You'll never guess where that was."

"The Romanov–von Baden castle?" Joe said automatically.

Frank was impressed. "Good guess." He nodded. "But the Nazis found out. They went to the castle, killed the Resistance fighters there, and seized the gold. That's how that brick wall in the castle courtyard got all those bullet holes in it. Only two of the Resistance fighters escaped."

Joe's blue eyes gleamed with excitement. "One of them's got to be van der Meer."

Frank nodded again and looked up from the book. "The other was our bullion dealer, Johannes Appel."

"Does it say what happened to the gold?" Joe asked.

Frank gave a hollow laugh and read the last line

aloud. " 'The stolen Dutch gold disappeared into the mists of history.' "

"Very specific," Joe said. "We'll have to check out that location."

Frank ignored his brother's sarcasm. "Do you think this could have been the information that Merissa found on van der Meer?"

"Maybe," Joe said slowly, "although it's not really incriminating. What gets me, though, is that we know that not all of the gold disappeared into the mists. Some of it, at least, ended up in Appel's hands."

Frank stretched. He was getting restless. "Let's say Merissa was right, and there is some sort of crime van der Meer is hiding, something that would cause a scandal. Maybe it's not only Appel, but van der Meer who's linked to the stolen gold."

"That would certainly help explain where he gets his money," Joe said. "And as Merissa said on the tape, it would be a major scandal. This country practically worships him."

Frank began gathering together the material he'd been reading. "Somehow, it figures that we'd start working on Nancy's case and wind up deeper into our own."

"We still don't have the answer to the big questions," Joe said. "Who murdered Johannes Appel and why? And just how much does Jaap van der Meer know about the missing gold?"

* * *

Trapped inside the old windmill, Nancy and George shivered from the plunging temperature. They had been in the mill over two hours, and now the damp, chilly air seemed to penetrate right to the bone. The wind howled against the ancient structure.

They huddled against the wall that seemed to have the fewest drafts of cold air. Nancy was still holding the flashlight, but she was trying not to use it because the batteries were almost worn out, and the beam was little more than a thin, yellow glow. Outside, darkness had fallen, and the night was pitch-black.

"Why don't they insulate these places?" George grumbled. "Or heat them?"

"I don't think you're supposed to spend the night in here," Nancy said, trying to keep her voice cheerful. She and George had searched for another exit but hadn't found one. They were stuck inside the windmill until someone let them out. Will we freeze to death before we starve to death? she wondered. At that point it seemed a toss-up.

"I just thought of something," George said. "Why don't we shine the flashlight out one of those narrow windows on the upper level? We can signal someone."

"Yeah, the grand duchess if she's watching," Nancy reminded her.

"Oh. Well, maybe that wouldn't be such a bad idea. She's bound to notice we're missing."

"The more I think about the grand duchess, the scarier she seems," Nancy said. "I'd prefer it if she didn't find out we were here." She hesitated. "Unless she already knows and ordered someone to lock us in."

"But why?" George asked. "I know she's made sure someone's with us constantly, but do you really think she'd lock us in?"

"I don't know," Nancy said. "But she seems so controlling, as if she's either suspicious of us or trying to keep us from finding out something. And if she *didn't* have anything to do with our getting locked in, I don't want her to know about it. She'll trust us even less."

"Then we wait until someone else finds us?"

"Maybe in the morning someone will pass by," Nancy said optimistically.

Nancy didn't know how long they waited before she thought she saw a brief glimmer of light beneath the door.

"What is it?" George asked.

"I'm not sure. I'm going upstairs to find out." Again Nancy climbed the shaky staircase and peered out a narrow window. Outside, the unmistakable beam of a flashlight bobbed toward them.

"Someone's coming," Nancy called down softly to George. She went back to the narrow window. A minute later she could actually make out the figure. "It's the castle's groundskeeper," she said. "Ot Schrijver."

George ran to the stout wooden door and

started pounding on it. "Help!" she shouted. "We're locked in the windmill."

Nancy saw the groundskeeper hurry toward the windmill. Seconds later as she descended the stairs, she heard the sound of a key.

The groundskeeper flung the door open, shining his light on the girls. "What are you two doing in here?" he demanded.

"We got locked in," Nancy said calmly. "How did you find us?"

"The grand duchess sent me to reset the sails," he replied in a gruff voice. His eyes narrowed. "You still haven't told me what you were doing here. Are you the ones who have been tampering with the sails?"

"Of course not!" George said indignantly.

"Why does the position of the sails matter?" Nancy asked, hoping he'd confirm her hunch that someone was using them to send messages to the castle.

Ot Schrijver glared darkly at Nancy and George. "The sails have to be positioned in different ways depending on where the wind is coming from," he explained. "If they are not set properly, the wind will blow right through them, and the windmill is useless. You may be guests in the castle, but you have no right to be out here."

"Why not?" George asked. "Isn't the windmill part of the castle grounds?"

"I'm warning you," the man said angrily. "The grand duchess has been upset about many things lately. Stay away from this windmill."

"What's upsetting her?" Nancy demanded.

"That is no business of yours," Schrijver shot back. He stared at them again, his eyes narrowed and his face stern. "If you hurry back, you'll just make dinner. Then I suggest you both leave here—unless you want to disappear just like your friend Merissa did!"

Chapter

Ten

Nancy awakened early the next morning, her thoughts troubled. She still had no idea who had locked her and George in the windmill—or why. The action had been deliberate; she was sure of that because it had been done so quietly. The question was, why. Was someone trying to keep them out of the way for a few hours? Or get them out of the way permanently? Which assumes that we are in someone's way, Nancy thought.

Ot Schrijver seemed the most likely suspect; she'd have to check him out. But most troubling of all was that Merissa had been missing for at least four days, if not longer. If she had been abducted, the kidnapping wasn't the sort in which the captors demanded a ransom. I hope she's still alive, Nancy thought.

Nancy shivered beneath the warmth of the down comforter. Although it was barely six, she got out of bed and dressed in a warm sweater and jeans. Breakfast in the castle was served between seven and eight, which meant that things should be quiet. This was a good time, she thought, to look for a way into the windowless tower.

Nancy opened her door and blinked. George was sitting in the hallway outside her room, reading a paperback.

"George," Nancy said, "what are you doing?"

George gave her a wan smile. "I couldn't sleep. I kept thinking about Merissa. So I figured I'd just wait out here until you got up." George closed the book and stood. "Did you know Ot Schrijver lives in a cottage behind the castle?"

"That little stone building with the thatched roof on the other side of the forest?"

George nodded. "One of the maids told me last night, after we got back. I was thinking—"

Nancy laughed. "Great minds think alike. I'd love to get a look inside his cottage, too. Right now, though, I'd like to find that tower we noticed yesterday."

Together, the two friends moved quietly through the corridor toward the stairs. The castle was silent, and Nancy was beginning to think they were the only two people awake. As they reached the landing, however, she heard angry voices drifting up from the second floor.

She froze in place, silently raising her hand and motioning George to stop and listen. The voices were Andrei's and his grandmother's, and they were arguing.

"We both did what we had to do," the grand duchess said bitterly.

"Why didn't you tell me?" Andrei asked in an anguished voice.

Heavy footsteps sounded on the stairs from the first floor. Then a third voice interrupted the argument.

"You sent for me, madam?"

George looked at Nancy, her eyes widening. The third speaker was Ot Schrijver.

"Yes," the grand duchess said. "I want you to go into Amsterdam to do some errands and make some purchases for me." There was the sound of paper rustling. "Here, I have prepared a list for you."

"I will go at once," the groundskeeper replied.

"At least *someone* here does as I ask," the grand duchess said when Schrijver had left.

"You ask too much, Grandmother," Andrei replied curtly. His footsteps echoed in the hallway and faded down the staircase.

"This is our chance," George whispered to Nancy. "Ot will be in Amsterdam, and—"

Nancy nodded. They abandoned their search for the tower and left the castle by the small iron door and the footbridge again. When they reached the nearby pebbled lane that led across the fields to the windmill, Nancy looked back. A small van was turning onto the main highway to Amsterdam from the castle's drive. She was able to recognize Schrijver at the wheel.

"We'll have to make this fast," Nancy told George. "They'll be serving breakfast soon, and I don't want to have to explain to the grand duchess why we missed it."

George ran a hand through her short, dark hair. "Let's hope the lock on Ot's door is easy to pick and that he doesn't have a wife or kids inside."

Ot's cottage was set in a grove of trees on the far side of the forest. Nancy and George followed a footpath that led off the pebbled lane and went past an old stone barn. They could see the small, one-story cottage only a little farther ahead, its pale thatched roof almost exactly the color of the dried winter grasses. A thin gray line of smoke rose from a chimney.

"This place looks like it was a farmhouse once," George mused.

Nancy nodded. "Yeah, about five hundred years ago. The good thing is, it looks deserted." She stepped up to the cottage's heavy wooden door. She tried the knob and it turned, but the door was firmly locked. Nancy knelt to examine it.

"Do you have your lock pick?" George asked.

"That only works on locks made in the last fifty years or so," Nancy said. "I'd need a skeleton key for this."

Undiscouraged, she walked around the side of

the cottage. A slanted wooden storm door led to a cellar of some sort. "It's probably locked from inside," George said to Nancy.

"We may as well try." Nancy lifted the latch on the storm door. To her surprise the door swung open.

Steep steps led down into a dark, narrow root cellar. Nancy entered the cellar cautiously, wishing she had her penlight with her. George joined her a moment later. They both stood in the darkness a moment, waiting for their eyes to adjust.

"Look," Nancy said. "I think there's a door in that wall. It must lead to the rest of the cellar."

The door did indeed open into the main cellar. They followed a rickety wooden stairway up into the house itself.

The smell of wood smoke filled Ot Schrijver's home. Although the cottage was small, each room had a hearth, and in the living room a fire still smoldered. The old-fashioned wooden furniture was big and heavy. Everything was as neat as a pin.

Nancy glanced in at a bedroom so narrow, there was barely room for more than the bed, a chest of drawers, and a bedside table. In the cramped kitchen dried herbs hung from the ceiling. The living room, which was the biggest room of all, held only two hard-backed wooden chairs at angles to the fireplace, a heavy bookcase, and several tables.

"Not exactly like living at the castle," George observed.

"No," Nancy agreed. She looked around her. "I think we can safely say that Ot is a neat man. Everything here is in its place and spotless."

"He likes flowers and plants," George said, nodding toward a stack of books on gardening on a side table in the living room. "I guess that makes sense for a groundskeeper."

"Look at this," Nancy said. Also on the table was a framed black-and-white photograph of a couple with a young boy about the age of ten. She picked it up and looked at it. The photograph was obviously old and was faded. Curious, she turned it over. On the cardboard backing she saw that someone had written the date 1944 in the lower right-hand corner.

George slid open the drawer in the side table. For a moment Nancy thought she caught a glimpse of coins and colorful ribbons.

"War medals," George said. "Like the ones we saw at Jaap's."

Nancy set the photograph back in its place and picked up a yellowed parchment certificate written in Dutch. A royal coat of arms was at the top.

"That looks official," George commented, looking at the document over Nancy's shoulder.

Nancy nodded. "And dated 1946." She pointed to the line where a name had been filled in. "But the name is Blankert, not Schrijver."

"His mother's maiden name?" George suggested.

Nancy shook her head. "Who knows." She slipped a pen and small notepad from her jeans pocket and carefully wrote down the Dutch words from the certificate. "Maybe we can get Mevrouw Wouters or someone to translate this for us."

"Good idea," George said.

Nancy put the document back in exactly the position she'd found it. Then she tried to close the drawer. It stuck and she pushed harder. Then it closed with such a bang that the top book in the pile, a book on roses, flew off the table. A folded piece of paper fluttered from the pages. Nancy reached for it and unfolded it.

"Some sort of receipt dated three days ago." Carefully she copied down the words on the receipt, then picked up the book, put the receipt back in it, and carefully put the book back on top of the pile.

George looked around. "Have we seen everything?"

"Enough for now," Nancy answered, glancing at her wristwatch. "We'd better make our appearance at breakfast before they notice we're missing."

As the girls headed back to the castle, Nancy saw a small delivery truck drive through the castle gates. Instead of entering the courtyard, it circled the fortress and parked beside the footbridge that led to the metal door. The delivery man got out and began to unload boxes of groceries from the back.

Nancy called out, "Excuse me, do you speak English?"

The delivery man, a big, blond fellow with a wide smile, nodded. "Yes, of course," he said in barely accented English.

"Could you possibly translate something for us?" Nancy asked. She held out the little notepad where she'd copied the words from the government document.

The delivery man furrowed his brow and read through the words. "It is a commendation from the Dutch government for two Resistance fighters who were awarded medals for bravery in World War Two. But they were killed in the war, too." He pointed to the page. "They were killed in 1944."

"Really?" Nancy said with exaggerated innocence. She flipped the page in the notepad to where she'd copied the words from the receipt. "And what about this?"

"It says, 'blue china monkey,'" the delivery man said, jabbing a thick finger at the words.

"No kidding," George said, glancing at Nancy with a knowing expression on her face.

Nancy thanked the man, who regarded her quizzically for a moment, as if wondering why she would ask him to translate such strange notes. Then he went back to unloading boxes. Nancy and George crossed the footbridge and entered the castle.

"So," Nancy said quietly when they were inside. "Ot bought that blue china monkey. He must have been the one who sent it to the grand duchess."

"Do you think he knew it would upset her?" George asked.

"I'm not sure," Nancy admitted. "When he let us out of the windmill, he seemed very protective of her. It's hard to imagine him deliberately trying to shake her that way."

"What did you think of that photograph and the war commendation?" George asked.

"It makes me wonder who the Blankerts were," Nancy said. "And what connection they have to Ot Schrijver."

Nancy and George climbed the servants' staircase to the second floor and entered the long hallway. They were about to head for the dining room when they saw the grand duchess descending the staircase from the floor above. Andrei and Emma were on either side of her.

Suddenly a maid rushed up the staircase from below, almost hysterical.

"Madam, you must come at once!" she cried.

"What's wrong, Karin?" the duchess asked gently.

"The—the courtyard," the maid stammered. "The wall—"

"What about it?" Emma demanded.

Nancy watched the maid choke back tears.

Andrei put a comforting hand on the servant's shoulder. "Show us, Karin," he told her.

Nancy and George joined Andrei, Emma, and the grand duchess as they trailed the sobbing maid downstairs into the great hall and outside. Karin pointed to the bullet-pocked brick wall where, some fifty years earlier, the eight Resistance fighters had been shot by Nazis.

Nancy fought back a feeling of shock when she saw what had upset the maid. The wall was spattered with eight dark red stains that ran down the bricks and pooled on the cobblestones.

"Blood!" George exclaimed, stunned.

Chapter

Eleven

Nancy saw the color drain from the grand duchess's face. The elderly woman leaned against Andrei for support. "Not again," she murmured. "It can't happen again."

Andrei put his arm around his grandmother and drew her close. He, too, Nancy noticed, looked stunned. Beside him Emma stood with clenched fists, her face a tight mask of fear.

Nancy walked across the cobblestones to examine the wall. Shuddering a little, she knelt and dipped one finger in a pool of blood. A feeling of relief went through her as she realized what the thick red liquid really was.

"It's stage blood," she told the others. "Food coloring, cornstarch, and water. It's a trick set up to frighten you."

"Why would someone do this?" Emma demanded in an offended tone.

The grand duchess let go of Andrei, anger flashing in her eyes. "This is a cruel prank," she declared. "Who would do such a thing!" She turned to the maid. "Karin, please clean this up at once."

"Yes, madam," the maid said.

"I will know who is causing such disturbances in my household," the grand duchess announced. Nancy saw her eyes flicker suspiciously at her and George.

"Maybe it's the same person who sent you the blue monkey," Nancy suggested.

The elderly woman regarded her shrewdly. "And who would that be?"

"Perhaps your groundskeeper, Ot Schrijver," Nancy suggested, wondering as she spoke what the reaction would be.

"That's absurd," Andrei said at once. "Ot has worked for our family for several years. His loyalty is beyond question."

"Of course it is," Emma joined in. "There's no one more trustworthy than Ot."

"You may all be in danger," Nancy said quietly. "I think you have to question yourselves about even the people you trust most."

"We will do nothing of the kind," the grand duchess said. "As our servants are loyal to us, we are loyal to them. Now, we will have no more discussion of this matter." She favored Nancy with a gracious smile. "Come inside, all of you. Our breakfast is waiting."

Breakfast was calm, if somewhat tense. The bloody wall wasn't mentioned. Nancy marveled that all three of the Romanov–von Badens acted as if it had never happened.

"And what are your plans for today?" the grand duchess asked Nancy and George.

"This afternoon we're meeting Frank and Joe, our friends from America," George told her.

Andrei helped himself to another serving of smoked salmon. "I hope you're meeting them someplace that's fun."

"Club Paradiso, in the city," Nancy said, wondering if the prince would recognize it.

"A favorite of mine," Andrei told her approvingly. "It's an old church that's been converted into a dance club. In the afternoons they often have free concerts for the young people of Amsterdam."

"I don't know if we have an extra car available to take you into the city this afternoon," the grand duchess said thoughtfully. "Ot and Pieter are both running errands for me."

She brightened and looked at her grandson. "Andrei, will you be good enough to take them into Amsterdam? Emma can go with you, and you can all go to the club together."

"Please say yes, Andrei," Emma chimed in immediately. "It's been ages since I went to a club. It would be so much fun."

Andrei's eyes went from his grandmother to his sister, then with an elegant shrug of defeat he smiled at Nancy and George. "I am at your service," he told them.

Nancy smiled back, but her eyes met George's, and she knew they were thinking the same thing. What they had to do was get away from this castle and the Romanov–von Badens and find Merissa. And once again they were being controlled by the grand duchess.

Nancy clung to the backseat of the Porsche as Andrei took a highway curve at his usual grand prix speed. Beside her, Emma looked annoyed. In the front seat George looked slightly sick.

"Andrei, slow down!" Emma ordered.

"Stop worrying," Andrei said in a soothing voice. "Why don't you look behind you? The sunlight on the trees is beautiful."

Not wanting to get into the argument, Nancy did as he suggested. Afternoon sun shone on a stand of elm trees, coating their bark in a wintry silver light. Then something else caught her eye—a black sedan behind them, being driven at a speed nearly equal to Andrei's. She watched it closely and made out a man with a reddish beard at the wheel.

Someone's following us! Nancy thought. She wondered if she should mention it to the others, but some instinct warned her not to. She liked both Andrei and Emma, but she had a case to solve, and she knew the only ones she could fully trust were George, Frank, and Joe.

As Andrei reached the outskirts of the city Nancy periodically checked out the back window. Each time she saw the black sedan traveling one or two cars behind them. It was only when they were in the heart of the old part of Amsterdam that the black sedan turned off onto one of the low bridges that spanned the canals and disappeared.

"Amsterdam is getting worse than New York," Andrei muttered as he drove alongside one of the canals. "There's no parking anywhere."

"You could just drop us off," George suggested.

"No, I will find a space," the prince assured them.

Seconds later he pulled into a spot beside the water. Nancy gazed out over the now-familiar sight of the crowded canal. Houseboats and barges were anchored along the sides.

"We're only a few blocks from the club!" Andrei announced triumphantly as they all got out of the car, and he locked it.

Emma frowned at him. "And the ground beneath us is sloping toward the water. This is an illegal space, Andrei. You know you shouldn't park here."

"Let me worry about that," her brother replied with genuine annoyance.

Nancy pulled her collar up against the cold as

they started to walk away from the car. A frigid wind cut across the water.

"I will have Pieter drive us back," Emma announced in a huffy tone.

George was trailing behind Nancy. "Omigosh!" she exclaimed, her dark eyes growing wide. The expensive red Porsche was rolling toward the canal. "You may have to."

The whole group turned, but before anyone could move, the car rolled over the edge and slid front-first into the murky water. With a loud sucking *glop,* the shiny red car sank from view.

Andrei glared at his sister as if it were her fault. "Don't say it," he warned.

"You didn't put on the parking brake, did you?" Emma asked in an exasperated tone. Her bright blue eyes were laughing, however.

"No, I was too busy being angry at you."

"Uh—what do we do now?" George asked, clearly wanting to prevent an argument.

"I will have to have the car pulled out," Andrei answered, his face flushed with embarrassment.

"I'll call a tow service, Andrei," Emma offered in a conciliatory tone. "You stay here with the car." She turned to Nancy and George. "You two had better go meet Joe and Frank. When you're ready to return to the castle, just call. Grandmama will have someone pick you up."

Nancy and George left Emma and her brother by the side of the canal.

"I can't believe it," George said as they set off

for the club. "Free at last! We're actually without an escort."

"Thanks to Andrei," Nancy agreed, grinning. "I thought I'd go crazy this morning just waiting to go into the city."

They soon found Club Paradiso in a huge, hundred-year-old church on a canal at the edge of Amsterdam's old city. The grand brick building had been painted white on the outside, but on the inside, the walls were a bright and gaudy red with wild, graffitilike designs.

The lobby was packed with young Amsterdammers and a surprising number of young Americans. Nancy smiled as she heard traces of New York City accents and others that could only be from the South.

On the stage, in the part of the church where the altar used to be, a rock band was playing a hard-driving set that had nearly everyone on their feet, dancing frenetically.

Nancy felt her own body swaying to the music. She nodded toward the far corner of the high-ceilinged room. "I think I see Frank!" she shouted to George over the music.

The two girls made their way across the crowded floor, though not without each of them being pulled into the dance at least once. Nancy found herself dancing with a good-looking young man with red hair. "American?" he asked.

Nancy nodded, having too much fun dancing to talk. After a couple of minutes she began dancing her way toward the Hardys.

"You must come back here," the young man said.

"I'll try," she promised before spinning away. At last she and George reached the Hardys.

"Where's Emma?" Joe asked, looking disappointed.

"Helping her brother get his car out of the canal," Nancy answered when there was a break in the music. "Did you find what you were looking for—anything connected to the man who appeared at the castle?"

"Nothing," Frank reported. "And I think I've talked to everyone here who speaks English."

Joe nodded toward the crowd. "Take a look. The problem is half the guys in Amsterdam seem to have brown hair and wear worn, black leather jackets. Whenever we describe our suspect, people tell us, 'Lots of people look like that.'"

The band started in again at an ear-shattering decibel level. "Can we go somewhere where we don't have to shout?" Nancy asked.

"There's a café at the American Hotel just down the street," Frank said. He led the way back across the room to the entrance.

Halfway across the dance floor Nancy froze. She spotted a bearded man at the counter where soft drinks were being served. He was staring at his drink, but Nancy couldn't help feeling that he had been looking at her. She was certain it was the same man who had followed them into Amsterdam in the black sedan. The sooner she got out of the club, the better she'd feel.

When the Hardys, George, and Nancy were in the lobby, Nancy told the others about the man.

"Let's split up," Joe suggested. "Nancy and George can walk ahead while Frank and I hang back. That way, we can see if the guy with the beard follows you or not."

On the street Nancy and George walked toward the nearby Leidsestraat, a shopping street crowded with pedestrians. The American Hotel, a fairy-talelike building of yellow brick, with slender towers, little balconies, and curved windows, faced a busy square filled with traffic.

Nancy and George entered the elegant café on the ground floor. It was a high-ceilinged room, with murals painted on the walls, and huge chandeliers of stained glass.

They took a small marble-topped table near the window and ordered coffee and pastries. Ten minutes later Frank and Joe joined them and ordered hot chocolate.

"No trail," Frank reported. "You left the club clear."

"I'm not comforted," Nancy said. "Things at the castle are getting really bizarre." She told them about being locked in the windmill, finding the receipt for the blue monkey in Ot's cottage, and the fake blood on the wall that morning.

"Sounds as if someone's after the grand duchess or maybe even Andrei," Frank said thoughtfully.

Nancy nodded. "I'm wondering if it's the same

guy who killed Appel. Maybe he's stalking the Romanov–von Badens for some reason."

"What I want to know is if it's the same person who abducted Merissa," George said. "And that reminds me—Andrei never gave us a copy of the tape."

"You're right," Nancy said. "We'll have to ask him about it later." They paused in their conversation while a waiter set down cups of steaming hot chocolate. When he was gone, Frank spoke.

"Joe and I came across some interesting information at the library last night," he told them. "We might have even figured out what it was that Merissa learned about Jaap van der Meer. All the weird stuff that's been happening—I think it goes back to events fifty years ago."

Frank looked across the table at Nancy. "You might not believe this, but we may all be involved in the same case."

"You mean the gold bullion that was stolen during the war is connected to the Romanov–von Badens?" George asked.

Frank nodded. "Since they were losing the war, the Nazis decided to ship their stolen Dutch gold to Germany. But Dutch Resistance fighters, disguised as German soldiers, intercepted it. They snatched the gold right out from under the Nazis' noses. And guess where they took it for safekeeping." He paused. "The castle."

Nancy gasped, and George looked startled.

Joe picked up the story. "The only problem

was that somehow the Nazis found out where it was and decided to get it back."

"That's when they executed all those Resistance fighters against the wall," Nancy said. She could feel the pieces of the case coming together, only she still didn't quite know how they fit.

Joe took a sip of his hot chocolate. "Exactly," he said. He glanced at Frank, then back to Nancy and George. "That's not all. We found a list of the names of the Resistance fighters who were involved. There were ten of them. Eight were killed and two survived."

"Johannes Appel and Jaap van der Meer," Frank concluded.

"Incredible!" George murmured.

"What happened to the gold?" Nancy asked.

"That seems to be the billion-dollar question," Frank replied. "The gold disappeared—'into the mists of history,' according to what we read. Except it hasn't. Bit by bit, it's still turning up all over the world mixed in with other gold shipments."

"So it looks as if Appel made off with some of it," Nancy concluded.

"Or maybe," Frank added, excitement in his voice, "it was his payment for collaborating with the Nazis. Someone betrayed those Resistance fighters and told the Nazis where to find the gold that night. Only an insider could have done it."

"And I'll bet you anything Jaap van der Meer was in it up to his patriotic ears," Joe said in a disgusted tone.

George nodded. "It would certainly explain how he can afford a priceless art collection."

"Frank," Nancy said, "did you find a list of names of the Resistance fighters who died?"

Frank reached into his coat pocket and took out a photocopy of an article in one of the reference books. He handed it to Nancy, who skimmed it quickly.

She was unable to hold back her own excitement. "Two of the people who were executed were named Blankert—a married couple, Elsa and Max!"

"I wonder if they're the couple in the old photograph in Ot's cottage," George speculated.

"So somehow Ot Schrijver, the grand duchess, van der Meer, and Appel are all connected to the night when the gold disappeared," Joe said.

Nancy finished her coffee. "And that stunt with the blood is a definite link. It's as if that was some sort of reminder about what happened at the castle. But why?"

George sighed restlessly. "Let's get back to talking about Merissa. If she discovered all this and wrote about it, then the people of the Netherlands might discover that one of their greatest war heroes was really a traitor and possibly a thief."

"Exactly!" Joe said excitedly. "And the person who had the most to lose—who *had* to stop her—would be Jaap van der Meer. Otherwise, he would be destroyed."

"You really *did* see Merissa in the window of

Jaap's house, didn't you?" Nancy said slowly. "I feel terrible, George. I should have believed you."

"Yes, you should have," said George. "But what matters now is that we have to get back inside Jaap's house to free her. We've wasted a lot of time already."

Joe looked skeptical. "Getting in is easier said than done. Didn't you see those two bodyguards in his study yesterday?"

George gave a shrug. "So he has bodyguards. We've dealt with worse."

"We won't be helping Merissa if we get ourselves caught," Nancy pointed out. "What if we walk past his house on the opposite side of the canal? That way we can do some surveillance and come up with a solid plan."

"Let's do it now," George proposed.

They left the American Hotel and walked up the Leidsestraat to Dam Square, retracing their steps from a day earlier around the palace. A short while later the four friends were looking across the Singel Canal toward Jaap van der Meer's townhouse. The draperies were still drawn, but light crept between cracks in the draperies in several rooms on the ground floor.

Nancy squinted up at the garret window. The window glass was streaked but not grimy the way it had been the day before.

George stood next to her. "What do you see, Nancy?"

"I'm not sure. Maybe nothing." She was carrying a small shoulder bag with the strap across her chest, and she reached down and opened it. A few moments later she pulled out a small case and flipped it open. It was a pair of mini-binoculars. "I knew I brought these along for a reason," she said.

Putting the binoculars to her eyes, she adjusted the focus and zoomed in on the window. She gave a little gasp.

"What? What is it?" George asked.

"Yeah, what? I don't see anything," Joe Hardy said.

Nancy handed the binoculars to George. "See for yourself," she said. "Someone has written the letters *SOS* in the dirt on the window."

George looked through the binoculars. "You're right!" she exclaimed. "Well, that's good enough for me. Merissa must be up there." She handed the binoculars back to Nancy.

"Yes," Nancy said. "I just wish I had believed you yesterday." She put the binoculars away.

"Look!" Frank said, pointing at the house. Van der Meer and his two bodyguards were walking out the front door and heading toward a black car with tinted windows that was parked in front.

"It's now or never," George said. "We're going inside to rescue Merissa!"

Chapter

Twelve

NANCY WATCHED JAAP and his two bodyguards get into the black car and pull away from the townhouse.

"Who do you think is left inside?" Joe asked.

"The butler and maybe a cook or something," Frank said. "But if there are other servants, they're probably at the back of the house."

"The important thing is that those goons are gone," George pointed out.

"All I need is to get to the stairs," Nancy said.

"Joe and I can stand watch outside," Frank suggested, "in case van der Meer and his bodyguards come back."

Nancy turned to George. "Think we can get past the butler?"

"Definitely!" George replied. "No problem."

Joe looked at Frank. "If Nancy and George aren't out in fifteen minutes, I'm going in after them."

"You got that right," Frank affirmed. He turned to Nancy and George. "Is that enough time?"

Nancy considered a moment. "Well, it's enough time to get in and get out," she said slowly. "And enough time to get into serious trouble if anything goes wrong."

Frank gave her a rueful smile. "I guess it's going to be one or the other, isn't it?"

Nancy nodded.

"I'm just wondering how we're going to get upstairs to the top floor," George said, glancing up at the elegant five-story townhouse.

"Leave that to me," Nancy told her. "You just make sure the butler is too busy to stop me."

George nodded. "Deal."

Nancy and George climbed the stone steps and rang the bell. The great wooden door swung open, and the elderly butler stood in the entrance. He looked surprised to see them.

"Mijnheer van der Meer is not—"

"We're so sorry to bother you today," Nancy interrupted, pushing past him into the elegant hallway. "I lost an earring when I was here yesterday, and I know exactly where it is."

Before the flustered servant could stop Nancy, she was racing toward the grand staircase.

"But you can't—" The worried butler moved toward the staircase, but George blocked him.

"This painting," she said, pointing to one of the oils on the wall. "Is this one of the Rembrandts or is this a Vermeer? I can't remember."

"It's a van Gogh," the white-haired servant growled.

Nancy, at the top of the first flight of stairs, hesitated as she heard the butler picking up a telephone receiver and speaking in rapid Dutch.

She turned in time to see George dive for him, reaching out to grab the telephone from his hands.

"You are too late," the butler said, his eyes panicked and his face red with fear. "I have alerted Mijnheer van der Meer."

George turned and raced after Nancy.

"The butler went for the telephone," she shouted, catching up to her when she was halfway up the staircase to the third floor. "He alerted van der Meer, I guess on his car phone."

"We have to hurry!" Nancy exclaimed.

They climbed rapidly up the flights of stairs, each one steeper and narrower than the one before. Finally they reached a set of ladderlike steps that led to the attic. At the top a stout wooden door was bolted tightly with several old, cast-iron sliding bolts. Nancy slid them aside one by one and pushed the door open. She and George rushed inside the darkened room.

They were in a low, dark space, with old wooden ceiling beams slanting just above their heads. The room had the smell of dust and cobwebs, and a thin, gray light filtered through the small circular window in the front gable. As they had seen outside, the letters *SOS* had been shakily drawn in the dirt on the window. From the inside the *S*'s were reversed.

Nancy's eyes adjusted to the dim light. An immense, ancient wardrobe loomed beside her, covered with cobwebs. Directly across from it, on a narrow cot under the eaves, a young woman slept, covered by a thin blanket. Her skin was pale, her long blond hair unkempt.

"Merissa!" George exclaimed in horror, rushing to her unconscious friend's side.

Outside van der Meer's house, Frank and Joe sauntered on the street, each of them glancing frequently at the house and alert for any sign of activity or commotion.

"I don't think I can wait fifteen minutes," Joe muttered. "I'm real nervous about Nancy and George going in there."

"Well, you won't have to wait," Frank said sharply, looking past Joe's shoulder. "Van der Meer's back!"

Joe turned and saw the black Mercedes with the tinted gray windows careening over the cobblestones. "What now?"

"We stall them any way we can."

The car screeched to a halt in front of the townhouse. Three doors opened, like wings sprouting from a great black bug. Van der Meer stepped from the back and spotted the Hardys immediately. Then his bodyguards emerged, the tall, thin one from the driver's side, the stocky one from the other side.

"I'll take the refrigerator in the dark suit," Joe muttered, tensing his body.

"He's all yours," Frank replied.

Van der Meer strode forward, slowly stripping off his black kid gloves. Joe observed the art collector's black wool coat and the white silk scarf draped casually around his neck. He stopped when he was several feet away from them.

"Greetings, dudes," Joe said. His lighthearted smile was betrayed by the coldness of his voice. "We just stopped by to ask you a few questions about that pricey art collection of yours."

"Yes?" Van der Meer's voice was even colder than Joe's.

Frank stepped forward. "We were wondering if we could take a look at the Vermeers again. See, I was thinking that maybe I'd write a paper on them for my history class, and—"

"Excuse me," Jaap said brusquely, "but I'm afraid this is not the time. Perhaps another day."

"We keeping you from something?" Joe asked innocently.

Van der Meer eyed Joe like a specimen under a microscope. Then he turned his eyes on Frank. He was completely unruffled, his face confident, his white hair lending him an aura of distinction.

"As a matter of fact, I have a business appointment." Van der Meer seemed to notice something on the sleeve of his wool coat. He lifted a hand and casually brushed it away. "I might add," he continued, "that whatever your two foolish friends are up to, they have made a very big mistake."

Joe gave a forced laugh and looked at Frank. Frank shrugged. "We don't know what you're talking about."

Barely glancing at the Hardys, van der Meer flicked his leather gloves casually over one shoulder. Frank saw the two goons' eyes meet across the roof of the black car. They started forward.

Van der Meer backed toward the steps of his townhouse. The butler appeared at the front door, his face white with panic.

"Keep them here," van der Meer ordered his men, his eyes glued on Frank and Joe. "I'll deal with them after I finish with the other two inside."

Van der Meer quickly walked up the steps of the townhouse. Frank barely had time to see him disappear into the house when the two goons rushed the Hardys like linebackers.

In the attic George knelt by the cot, shaking Merissa gently and murmuring her name. Her friend moaned faintly but didn't respond. She seemed to be in a deep, impenetrable sleep.

Nancy grabbed Merissa's wrist and felt for a pulse, watching her chest rise and fall slowly. The sleeping girl was barely breathing! Her pulse was strong but slow.

"I think she's been drugged," Nancy told

George. "Come on, we have to get her out of here fast!"

Nancy put her arm under Merissa's back and pulled her up, shaking her and repeating her name.

"Here's some water." George grabbed an enamel pitcher from a small table near the cot. For lack of a rag, she put her hand in the water and pressed it, cool and wet, gently against Merissa's cheeks and forehead. The unconscious girl's eyes fluttered. Her chest rose, and she seemed to fight for air.

"Come on, Merissa!" Nancy urged.

Merissa's eyes opened. She gazed at the two girls, blankly and without recognition.

"Merissa, it's me! George!"

"Help me get her up," Nancy ordered. "We'll have to carry her." Just then she saw Merissa's eyes begin to focus on George. Her eyelids blinked open and shut, as if she were fighting to stay awake.

"George," Merissa said so weakly she was almost inaudible. "You've finally come." Then her eyes closed and she slumped.

"Merissa!" Nancy shook her again. "We're getting you out of here."

Suddenly Nancy heard shouts downstairs. Violent thuds vibrated up through the wood of the ancient house. She caught the alarm in George's eyes, but before either could say anything, footsteps thundered on the stairs below!

Chapter

Thirteen

N<small>ANCY RACED</small> to the entrance of the attic and slammed the wooden door shut. She spotted the dark hulk of the old armoire in the shadows. "Quick! Let's block the door!"

As the footsteps on the stairs grew louder, George rushed to help Nancy. The massive armoire was solidly built and heavy. With a screech it slid across the floor and blocked the entrance.

Seconds later the attic door opened and smacked against the back of the armoire. The ancient piece of furniture teetered but didn't budge.

"You'll never get away with this!" van der Meer shouted, his voice filled with rage. "In fact, you'll never get away at all!"

Nancy and George heard the attic door slam shut and the metallic clicking of the iron bolts as they were slid closed. Then they heard van der Meer's footsteps descending the staircase.

"Now what?" George asked in the silence that followed. "We're trapped."

Nancy shook her head. "There's still one way out." She picked up the small pedestal table beside Merissa's cot, strode to the small garret window and struck the table's legs against the glass. Shards of broken glass sprayed outside. Nancy chipped at jagged pieces until the frame was clear.

She dropped the table and went back to the cot, where she threw back the thin blanket. Merissa was wearing jeans, a wool sweater, and thick wool socks, but there was no sign of her shoes. Nancy helped George lift her to her feet. They stood on either side of her, holding her arms around their shoulders and supporting her at the waist. Merissa moaned faintly and tried to raise her head.

"She's coming out of it," Nancy said, feeling Merissa try to support herself on her own feet, then slumping in their arms again. "I'll climb out first. You can hand Merissa to me."

"Then where do we go—across the rooftops?" George looked dismayed. "They're not only covered with tile, they're steep. And Merissa can barely stand."

"We have more of a chance out there than we

do in here," Nancy told her. "Van der Meer will be back any minute!"

The thugs came toward Frank and Joe like a pair of bulldozers in trench coats.

"Let's lead them away from here and circle back," Frank said quickly.

"Good plan," Joe muttered. The brothers spun around and ran flat out for the street at the end of the block, where a narrow bridge arched across the canal. Frank heard the bodyguards shout and the sound of their shoes slapping against the cobblestones.

Joe briefly glanced over his shoulder. The two goons were gaining. And behind the men he saw a black car turning the corner.

"Move it!" Frank shouted. As the brothers approached the cross street, several bicyclists pedaled past and crossed the bridge over the canal. Frank heard the sound of grinding steel. A long, bright yellow streetcar swooped rapidly toward the bridge on its metal rails. It was just the cover he and Joe needed.

"Quick!" he cried, running into the street with Joe right beside him. The conductor began to clang his warning bell as the two Hardys raced across the rail in front of the streetcar to the other side of the street. The streetcar slowly rattled through the intersection on its great steel wheels, filling the intersection and hiding Frank and Joe from their pursuers.

Joe grabbed Frank's jacket. "I'll lead them into that square in front of the palace, where I can get lost in the crowd," he told Frank. "You hide and double back to help Nancy!"

The streetcar still concealed them from Jaap's goons. With a quick nod at Joe, Frank vaulted over the iron fence bordering the canal. The streetcar was halfway across the bridge, with the tail end about to clear the intersection. At any second Jaap's bodyguards would burst into the intersection and see them.

Frank lowered himself, dropping toward the canal until he could not be seen from street level. He gripped the cold steel bar of the fence tightly with his bare hands. The cold, dirty water rolled only a few feet below him.

Joe ran across the bridge alongside the streetcar. He measured his pace, using the streetcar for cover until he was across the intersection. The back of the Royal Palace loomed farther up the street ahead of him. Joe remembered that the palace fronted Dam Square, and the square was always filled with tourists. He knew he could lose his pursuers there in the crowd.

The streetcar gained speed and surged ahead of him. Joe looked back across the bridge and saw Jaap's goons on the other side. They spotted him at the same moment. The stocky one shouted angrily, and they ran toward him.

It was exactly what Joe wanted. He paused just a few seconds to give them time to catch up.

"Come on, boys," he said quietly, watching the two bodyguards race across the bridge. "Let's go on a wild-goose chase."

Nancy and George walked Merissa over to the window. George held her near-unconscious friend, while Nancy set the table under the broken window and climbed up on it.

Carefully avoiding sharp splinters of wood and broken glass, Nancy pulled herself through the opening. She stood on a narrow strip of roof between the attic window and the rain gutter that ran along the edge. The rooftop view of Amsterdam was dizzying. She took a deep breath to steady herself.

A raw, cold wind from the North Sea went straight through her wool jacket. She peered over the edge of the roof and quickly drew back. Five stories below, Jaap van der Meer was pacing back and forth in front of the house. Frank and Joe were nowhere to be seen.

The roof of van der Meer's townhouse was made of slate and rose in gentle angles on four sides to a flat, level rectangular area in the center. But the townhouse abutted the steep gables of the high-peaked, red tile roofs of houses on either side. In the rear a courtyard divided by stone walls into small, elaborate gardens ran along the entire back of the block.

Nancy spotted a narrow balcony facing the courtyard on the fourth floor of the house at the corner. It was an eight-foot drop from the roof. Glass doors led into someone's apartment. It was the only way out.

Nancy moved back to the attic window, where George waited with Merissa slumped against her. The blond girl was looking at Nancy, her gaze more alert.

"Here, hand her to me," Nancy told George. She stooped and reached in the window. George maneuvered Merissa into Nancy's arms and helped Nancy lift her outside.

Nancy hoisted Merissa up and tried to help her away from the edge of the roof while George scrambled out the attic window. Merissa seemed to suddenly regain consciousness, glancing at Nancy, then down at the dizzying five-story drop beside her. She gasped, as if she were fighting for air. Nancy felt her begin to topple.

"I've got you!" Nancy grabbed Merissa, spinning her around to face away from the edge. Merissa dug her fingers into Nancy's jacket, and her eyes were wide with fear.

Nancy took a deep breath. That had been a close call, and her heart was racing. She pointed to the balcony three houses away and tried to speak calmly. "If we can get over there, we can jump down and call the police from inside."

George looked at the steep tile roofs doubtfully. "Crossing these roofs is going to be like climbing up and down a giant zigzag."

"I can do it," Merissa said with a sudden

strength that surprised Nancy. "We have to. Our lives are at stake!"

Frank clung to the bottom rail of the iron fence, the cold metal numbing his hands. He gritted his teeth. He didn't think he could hold on much longer, but if he let go, he'd fall into the freezing water. He twisted his neck and looked at the bridge and saw the two bodyguards racing across it in pursuit of Joe.

Now Frank knew the coast was clear for him to double back to Jaap's house. "Good work, bro," he said softly, pulling himself up and over the fence.

He raced toward the intersection just as a black sedan careened around the corner and over the bridge in the direction of Joe's escape.

Frank started to circle around the block and approach Jaap's house from the other direction. He raced along the street, the cobblestones slippery with the late afternoon condensation. Afternoon was giving way to the early darkness of the Dutch city, and the long, lingering twilight had begun.

Passing a side street, Frank noticed a long, thick rope hanging from the joist beam of an old house. It was the house where they had seen furniture being moved a day earlier, right around the corner from van der Meer's.

Frank ran toward the Singel. He turned the corner—and froze. Jaap van der Meer was pacing impatiently in front of his house.

Frank darted back around the corner out of sight. He's waiting for his bodyguards, Frank thought, flattening himself against the house.

The steep, tiled roofs were difficult going for George and Nancy, especially with a half-conscious person in tow. Moving cautiously on her hands and knees, Nancy climbed toward the peak of the first roof. Fortunately, her sneakers gave good traction against the red tile. She was glad that she had decided to dress casually that day.

As she climbed higher, the aerial view of Amsterdam's red tile roofs opened before her, the peaks, gables, and oddly shaped chimneys, the delicate church steeples jutting above them. Like a vision from a fairy tale, Nancy thought. And we're fleeing from the ogre.

At the peak of the roof she balanced herself carefully on the thick tile rim. George hoisted Merissa, who stretched her arms up the roof toward Nancy.

Nancy reached down and grabbed Merissa's hands. She pulled her up with George boosting from below. A moment later Merissa reached the top and sagged against Nancy.

"I guess I'm not as strong as I thought," she murmured, struggling to catch her breath.

"You're doing fine," Nancy told her.

George reached the peak of the roof. "At least going down the other side is a lot easier," she said. She pushed off and slid down the steep incline on the seat of her jeans, using her feet as brakes. When she reached the bottom, Nancy helped Merissa down into George's arms, then followed.

They repeated the process to get over the next roof, but this time it seemed to take forever. Nancy noticed that Merissa was clearly exhausted. Her spurt of energy was almost used up.

Nancy walked to the edge and looked down on the fourth-floor balcony below them. She had a much better view of the balcony now. Two wide glass windows and a glass door led inside, but the curtains were tightly drawn, and the door securely shut. No lights were on inside.

"Now what?" George asked as she crouched beside her. "We can't take a chance on jumping down there if that door is locked. And it doesn't look like anyone's at home."

"I know," Nancy said. She looked around. They were at the end of the block, where the row of zigzagging roofs turned abruptly left on the street that ran perpendicular to the Singel. The high, peaked gable rose above them like an A-frame, and next to it was a second gabled house. A rain gutter, two feet wide and seamed with tar, ran between the buildings.

"Wait here with Merissa," Nancy instructed. She stepped onto the rain gutter and walked to the front of the houses. The ornate curves of the old baroque facade rose above the A-shaped tile roof. Holding on to the facade where it projected beyond the actual roof, Nancy peered out.

A pulley hung from a strong iron hook that had been screwed into a thick beam, projecting horizontally from beneath the roof. A rope had been threaded through the pulley, and its two long ends snapped and billowed in the wind. Nancy realized it was the house where the family had been moving furniture.

She saw movement below. Gripping the edge of the facade tightly, Nancy looked down and saw Frank Hardy. She didn't dare shout to get his attention, in case Jaap or his men were nearby. Looking around, she noticed some of the tiles against the edge of the roof were cracked and broken. She picked up a piece and hurled it down.

Frank jumped back reflexively as the piece of tile fell almost directly in front of him. It smashed on the street, spraying across the cobblestones. But instead of looking up as Nancy hoped, Frank pressed closer to the side of the house.

"Come on, Frank!" Nancy murmured, tossing down more of the broken tile. As she watched impatiently, Frank dodged and weaved as the fragments rained down around him like little bombs.

Finally, when the bombardment stopped, Frank carefully looked up and saw Nancy waving from the edge of the roof. He raised a forefinger to his mouth and pointed to the corner.

High overhead, Nancy nodded that she understood. Frank was warning her to keep quiet.

Frank moved toward the house. Both ends of the long rope were tied to a hook that projected from the house. Quickly Frank undid the thick, loose knot. He flicked the rope, making it ripple up the length of the building and swing the pulley at the end of the roof joist.

On the roof Nancy heard the metallic grind of the steel pulley rubbing against the iron hook. She saw Frank swing the rope again, billowing it in her direction. With one hand gripping the facade, Nancy leaned out from the house and forced herself to ignore the deadly drop below. With her other hand she reached out and caught one end of the rope as it came toward her. Then she pulled herself back to safety, bringing the rope with her. She gave a sigh of relief.

George scrambled to the edge of the roof.

"Frank's down there," Nancy told her.

"Great, it's only a five-story drop," George muttered. "I'm not keen on jumping."

"We don't have to." Nancy showed her the rope. "Bring Merissa here. This is our way down."

George retreated back along the roof while Nancy looped the rope and knotted it. A moment later George helped Merissa over to Nancy. Although George supported her with one arm, Merissa had regained some strength and was walking almost on her own.

"Can you hang on to George piggyback-style?" Nancy asked.

Merissa nodded. "I—I think so," she said. "I know I can," she echoed in a firmer voice.

"George, put your foot into the loop," Nancy instructed.

George did as she was told. Nancy handed her the rest of the rope. "Now hang on to this tightly. And, Merissa, wrap your arms around George's neck and your legs around her waist. I'm going to help you off the roof, and Frank will lower you down."

When George and Merissa were ready, Nancy signaled Frank. He wrapped his end of the rope once around the hook projecting from the brick wall without knotting it, then held on. He watched George slowly and precariously maneuver herself off the edge of the roof, with Merissa clinging tightly to her back. The rope tightened and became taut, pulling hard against Frank's hands. Slowly he let it out. It turned neatly around the hook.

George let go of the roof and swung into space, her foot supported by the loop. Frank let out more rope, feeding it slowly through the overhead pulley. George and Merissa descended smoothly, and soon they were on the ground. They hugged each other with relief.

Quickly Frank hauled the looped end of the rope back up the pulley and whipped it. Five stories above, Nancy caught the loop and pulled it over to the side of the roof. She stuck her foot in it, gripped the rope, and pushed away.

Once again Frank let out the rope, lowering Nancy smoothly down the facade of the darkened house. Soon she was standing beside George and Merissa, a little shaky but smiling.

"I suppose you couldn't have tried something ordinary like the stairs," Frank teased.

"Too boring," Nancy said, giving him a quick hug. "Thanks for helping out."

"No problem." Frank dropped the end of the rope and moved to the corner. He glanced around it. Van der Meer was still pacing in front of the townhouse. As Frank returned to Nancy and George, he saw a taxi turning onto the street. He stepped into the street with his hand in the air and waved it down.

"I'm going to look for Joe," he told Nancy, handing her the key to his hotel room. "We're staying at the Hotel Doelen. Room three-seventy-four. I'll meet you there as soon as I find my brother."

Joe raced around the gray stone palace into Dam Square. He paused a moment, making certain that one of the bodyguards spotted him. Crowds gathered around the street musicians and strolled across the square, their arms laden with shopping bags from the Kalverstraat.

Joe headed for the center of the square and was rapidly lost in the crowd. He glimpsed the thin bodyguard standing by the palace, searching for a sign of him. He decided to make a wide circle across the square and around the other side of the palace to return to the Singel.

He barely reached the side of the palace, however, when he saw the short, stocky bodyguard searching the street, not twenty feet away. The goon spotted Joe at the same time and went for him.

Joe looked around quickly and saw a man standing near him with a bicycle. He grabbed it from the surprised man's hands, jumped on, and started pedaling across the square, the owner's shouts following him.

Joe swerved wildly to avoid a cluster of startled pedestrians, and a man playing a guitar fled from his path. He glanced over his shoulder.

The bicycle owner was racing after him, and two police officers had joined the chase. Farther back, he saw Jaap's bodyguards. They were watching the ruckus Joe had created and backing away. Then Joe saw a black car speeding around the corner of the palace, heading straight for him!

This is not optimal, Joe thought, forcing himself to pedal harder. The bike couldn't go that much faster, and the black car was gaining. Joe tried not to give in to panic, but he was beginning to wonder just how many seconds he had left.

Suddenly he heard a loud clanging and the sound of metal screeching against metal. He turned again, just in time to see a great yellow streetcar bearing down on top of him!

Chapter

Fourteen

JOE THREW HIMSELF SIDEWAYS, tumbling head over heels as the streetcar veered past. The bicycle rolled with him, and he landed in a tangle of frame and wheels. The two police officers and the bicycle owner were on him before he could get to his feet. The owner went for his bicycle, while the police grabbed Joe by the arms and pulled him up, speaking harshly in rapid Dutch.

"I'm sorry, I only speak English," Joe shouted. "I'm American!"

One of the police officers nodded, his face stern. "And Americans steal bicycles whenever they want?"

"Joe!"

Hearing his name, Joe looked around. He saw

Frank in front of the palace, racing across the cobblestones toward him.

"I think this American should be arrested!" the bicycle owner said angrily in English. He was shaking his finger at Joe. With his other hand he held his bicycle by the handlebars, moving it back and forth to test the wheels.

"See, it's working just fine," Joe told him.

Frank came to a halt beside Joe and turned to the policemen. "Officers, I think we can explain this—"

Frank broke off when he saw the black sedan that had been racing up the Singel from van der Meer's house screech to a stop beside the gathering. The door opened—and the man who'd fled from Appel's office and the castle courtyard stepped out.

Instinctively Frank tensed and grabbed Joe's sleeve, ready for danger.

The man looked straight at Frank and Joe. Before either Hardy could utter a word, he took a wallet from his leather jacket and flashed a silver badge. Almost immediately the police officers and the owner of the bicycle stepped back.

"Frank and Joe Hardy? Inspector Albert Don of the Dutch Security Service," he introduced himself, smiling pleasantly.

"Dutch Security Service?" Frank echoed.

"I believe we're working on the same case." Don glanced toward the irate cyclist. "And you are not making matters easier for me. Let me talk to the police and clear up this matter."

Frank and Joe watched the Dutch agent approach the policemen.

"Nancy and George are safe," Frank muttered quietly to Joe as soon as Don was out of earshot. "So is Merissa."

Joe's eyes grew wide. "They actually got her out?"

Frank nodded. "And whatever van der Meer's up to, he's ruthless."

The Hardys watched while a long conversation, entirely in Dutch, took place among the police, the cyclist, and Albert Don. A few minutes later the disgruntled owner mounted his bike and pedaled away while the police strolled back to their duties.

"Let me get this straight," Joe said to Albert Don. "You were part of the sting?"

"Not exactly," Don replied. "But I, too, am trying to recover the stolen gold. Obviously, the Dutch government is extremely interested in this matter, since technically the gold belongs to us. Perhaps the three of us need to have a conversation."

"You're on," Frank said. "I wouldn't miss your side of the story for the world."

Inspector Don laughed. "I know a café not far from here."

Albert Don drove them to a small coffee shop on a nearby street. The café was brightly lit, and its brick walls had been whitewashed and hung with photographs. They took a table at the back where they could talk in private, and ordered hot chocolate. It was brought to them in little glasses set in metal cups, with tiny biscuits on the side.

"Did you kill Appel?" Joe demanded abruptly.

Don shook his head. "I was sent to question Appel and found his body the same way you did. I phoned in a report of the murder to my superiors and was told to report back to headquarters. I was on my way there when we saw each other on the stairs."

"And you followed us afterward," Frank said accusingly.

Albert Don nodded. "I apologize for dumping you in the canal like that, but I didn't know who you were or how you were linked to Appel." Don's handsome face flushed with embarrassment. "And due to some unusually thick red tape—there is a great deal of high-level security surrounding this case—I'm afraid it was not until today that I was informed that you were working on a sting in cooperation with our government.

"Now you can tell me something," Don continued. "How is it I ran into you at the castle?"

"We could ask you the same thing," Frank countered.

"We've been investigating Jaap van der Meer and the Romanov–von Badens," Don said. "They're among Appel's business clients."

"Nancy Drew is a friend of ours from America," Frank explained in turn. "She's here with her friend George Fayne to visit another friend, a reporter for the *International Tribune,* Merissa Lang. Merissa is engaged to Prince Andrei."

"Except that Merissa disappeared," Joe concluded.

"Disappeared?" Don echoed. "What does that mean?"

Frank and Joe exchanged looks. Frank spoke first. "Basically it means that Jaap van der Meer abducted her and was keeping her prisoner in the attic of his townhouse." He added, "Until about half an hour ago."

"You've freed her?" Don said, astonished.

"Nancy and George did," Joe corrected him.

Don nodded slowly, as if he were mulling over information. "That's why there was all the commotion at van der Meer's house when I drove past today. I saw you running from his men."

"Now it's your turn," Frank prompted. "I don't believe you were at the castle just because the Romanov–von Badens were Johannes Appel's clients."

The Dutch agent was quiet, and Frank felt Don's eyes on him, making an assessment. Then he looked down, staring into his cup of hot chocolate, swirling the liquid around, deep in thought. Finally he looked across the table at them.

"You know about the gold stolen during the war? Nazis trapped the Resistance fighters at the castle and killed them."

"Then they took the gold," Frank finished.

"That's the official version of the story," Don agreed. "But I have my own suspicions."

"Like what?" Joe demanded.

"I don't think the gold ever left the castle."

Frank looked steadily at Albert Don. "You mean the Romanov–von Badens were actually involved in the theft?"

"They're in it up to their aristocratic ears," Don said succinctly. "At the very least, the grand duchess is. And if Jaap van der Meer kidnapped this woman, Merissa, then perhaps she found out something that she shouldn't have."

"Let's go ask her," Frank suggested.

Don looked startled. "You know where she is now?"

"We're supposed to rendezvous at our room at the Hotel Doelen," Frank told him.

They paid for their hot chocolate, and Don drove them the short distance to the hotel.

Inside the Hardys' room, Nancy, George, and Merissa were waiting anxiously. Merissa was recovering quickly from her ordeal. She had used the bathroom to freshen up. Now her long blond hair was combed out, and her green eyes were alert.

Frank made introductions. Albert Don shook hands with Nancy and George.

"In a sense I've already met you," the agent told them.

Nancy looked at him curiously. "I don't think so," she said.

"Not knowing who you were, I've had you under surveillance for several days."

Nancy gazed at Don, and a look of disbelief filled her eyes. "Do you drive a black sedan?"

"Sometimes."

"You were the one with the red beard," she said, astonished. "You followed us into Amsterdam today and then to the Paradiso!"

Don nodded. "Yes, I hope this does not offend you. It was my duty to investigate the Romanov–von Badens and anyone connected with them."

George looked at Nancy and grinned. "We'd have done the same thing, given half a chance."

Don turned to Merissa. "Now I would like to hear your story."

Merissa shook her head, as if trying to wake from a bad dream. "Andrei took me to van der Meer's townhouse for dinner one night," she said in a quiet voice. "I was looking at some of the paintings when I noticed a gold ingot on his desk. It had a curious, old-fashioned stamp in it, and when I asked Jaap about it, he became very nervous." Merissa gave a little laugh. "I always knew my journalist's instincts would get me into trouble someday. I started digging. At the library I found a registry of gold bullion stamps, and I identified the one I had seen on the ingot on Jaap's desk. After some more investigation I learned it was part of a legendary cache of gold bullion."

Merissa paused, collecting her thoughts. "At

that point I researched the whole incredible story about what happened during the war. The Dutch Resistance had learned that the Nazis were taking the gold to Germany and decided to intercept it. The night the gold was stolen, they met at a tavern called the Blue Monkey—"

"That explains one thing," Nancy said, looking at George.

Merissa stopped, her eyebrows raised in question.

"Someone sent a blue china monkey to the grand duchess," George explained. "You should have seen the look on her face when she took it out of the box."

Merissa nodded, then continued her story. "The Resistance fighters signaled when the gold was coming through by changing the position of the sails on the windmills along the River Vecht."

"That's why the duchess keeps staring through that telescope at the windmill," Nancy said. "Someone must be setting the sails in that same position." Quickly she recounted what she and George had witnessed, including seeing the fake blood and being locked in the windmill. "It looks as if Ot Schrijver, the groundskeeper, is responsible," she concluded. "He's trying to scare her by reminding her of the past."

"The question is, why?" Frank said.

Merissa shrugged. "I have no idea how Schrijver is involved. I never came across anything in my research to link him to the theft of the gold and the killings afterward. I knew, of course, that van der Meer was one of the two survivors.

"A few days before you arrived, I stayed overnight at the castle," Merissa went on. "I couldn't sleep and decided to go for a walk. The library door was partly open. I heard voices, first the grand duchess's, then van der Meer's, which surprised me—I hadn't known he was at the castle. Then I realized they were arguing. And through the partly open door I saw a pile of gold bars on the table before them."

"The stolen gold!" Joe exclaimed.

Nancy saw that Albert Don's eyes were gleaming.

"You actually saw them with it!" The Dutch agent clenched his fist. "They're traitors, both of them!"

"What happened then?" George prompted.

Merissa's voice became stronger as she continued. "I was scared, but I knew this was the story of the century—at least for me it was. Every journalist dreams of getting one chance in a lifetime to bust something open, something big! And this was it, for me." She shrugged and looked at her friends apologetically. "I decided to eavesdrop."

Joe laughed. "Don't be sorry about it. You knew they were criminals."

Merissa nodded. "Sure, but I was about to expose my fiancé's grandmother. Anyway, van der Meer suddenly noticed the library door was open."

George drew in her breath sharply. "He saw you?"

"No," Merissa said. "You know those gigantic porcelain vases outside the library doors? I ducked behind one. He just looked out quickly and closed the door. I went back to my room."

"So why did he kidnap you?" Nancy asked.

"Because on the way back to my room I stumbled into one of van der Meer's body-guards," Merissa replied. She shivered. "Joost, the tall, thin one. He didn't say anything—he just looked at me. But he must have told Jaap he saw me coming from the library. I was working on the story in my apartment the next day when they came for me."

"That's when you hid the microcassette," George added.

"You found it!" Merissa exclaimed.

"Of course," George said. "Button, button—"

"Who's got the button?" Merissa finished, laughing. Suddenly she looked wistful. "Oh, George. Nancy. All of you. I can't tell you how good it feels to have friends like you."

Nancy smiled, relieved that they had success-fully rescued Merissa. "If George hadn't seen you at the attic window yesterday, you might still be a prisoner."

"They were giving me injections that made me sleep," Merissa said. "But sometimes the medication wore off. I knew Jaap had visitors yesterday because I could hear voices downstairs. So I forced myself to get up and go to the window. But it was only a few seconds before I lost consciousness and collapsed. Later I awoke again and was able to scribble SOS in the dirt on the window."

"The grand duchess was being so sweet to us," George said angrily. "And all the time terrible things were being done to you."

Nancy looked at George and nodded. "She must have known. It seems as if she and van der Meer are pretty close."

"Not just close," Merissa stated flatly.

"What do you mean?" Joe asked.

"She has the gold," Merissa replied.

A moment of stunned silence reigned.

Suddenly Nancy realized what Merissa was saying. "You mean it's in the castle?"

Merissa nodded. "And I know exactly where it's hidden!"

Chapter

Fifteen

T HAT WAS the other thing I saw through the library door," Merissa explained. "The bookshelf beside the fireplace on the right is a secret doorway, and it was open. I could see a staircase descending into darkness."

"Inside the windowless tower!" Nancy exclaimed.

Merissa nodded with surprise. "You noticed it? The next day when I went outside, I realized that the castle seemed to have an extra tower at the end of the library. But there were no rooms that I could remember, except the secret entrance beside the fireplace."

"Do you know how to open it?" Albert Don asked.

Merissa nodded. "I think so. The bookcase is

ornamented with heavily carved wood. At the top is a satyr's head with long horns. I noticed one of the horns was twisted sideways. It's only a hunch, but I bet that's it."

Albert Don stood up and began pacing the hotel room. "We must get in there and get that gold so we can prove it."

"Can't you have the police raid the castle?" Joe asked.

"It's not an easy matter," Don replied. "First of all, the castle is owned by exiled royalty, and they have many powerful friends, including Jaap van der Meer. As you know, many Dutch people consider him a patriot."

"For the time being," Frank added.

"It will be impossible to get a search warrant unless we have real evidence," Don told them.

"Let's go in and get it, then," Joe said.

"The castle's a fortress," Frank reminded him. "We'd never get in without being seen."

Nancy listened, her brow furrowed in thought. "I have an idea," she said slowly, looking at the Hardys and then Albert Don. "There's a small iron door at the back of the castle, and a footbridge over the moat that was added about a hundred years ago. Sometimes people making deliveries use it. If it was unlocked, we could get in and out unobserved."

"That's a pretty big if," Joe pointed out.

"Not if George and I go back to the castle for dinner and open it from the inside. Then you guys can slip in and open the secret passage in the library. If the gold is there, all you need to do is bring out a few bars."

"That will be enough to get a search warrant and make arrests," Albert Don agreed.

Frank shook his head. "Impossible. By now van der Meer will have told the grand duchess that you're onto him."

"Maybe," Nancy said. "But the grand duchess has no reason to think that we suspect *her* of anything. We could act as if nothing has happened. Even if it's a trap for us, it'll give you guys time to get in and out."

Albert Don looked soberly at Nancy. "If anything goes wrong, I can have the police at the castle in no time. Still, if van der Meer has told the duchess that you rescued Merissa this afternoon, she'll be a very dangerous enemy."

"I know the risks," Nancy said bravely. She looked at George. "What do you think?"

"I'm with you," George said. She looked at Merissa with concern. "What about you? What are you going to do now?"

"I'm not sure," Merissa replied. "I have to write this story, obviously. And when I do, it will probably mean the end of my engagement. I mean, what's Andrei going to think when I expose his grandmother and Jaap, who's practically an uncle to him?"

"Andrei ought to realize that they deserve to be exposed," Frank replied.

"Maybe," Merissa said sadly. "But I think this means I'll have to say goodbye to Andrei."

"Do you want to talk to him before we go in?" George asked.

Merissa shook her head. "No way. It's payback time for the duchess and van der Meer."

Nancy sat stiffly in the backseat of the grand duchess's car as Pieter sped along the highway from Amsterdam. Nancy and George had worked out the details of the plan with Albert Don and the Hardys, then left Merissa in the hotel to get some sleep. If all went as planned, the Hardys and Albert Don would soon meet them. Through the window Nancy could see the forest of thin trees that bordered the castle grounds.

Sitting beside her, George sent Nancy an apprehensive look as the castle towers came into view. Would they be able to pull off the plan that would expose Jaap van der Meer and the grand duchess? Or would Jaap have already exposed them?

The car turned onto the narrow brick bridge. The enormous iron gate was ominously closed. Ot Schrijver eyed the two Americans suspiciously and opened the gate for the car. Then he shut it behind them with a resounding clang.

"Into the lion's den," Nancy whispered.

George let out a long breath. "And they're locking us inside the cage."

Pieter crossed the wooden drawbridge over the moat and entered the cobblestoned courtyard. He stopped the car in front of the wide steps that led to the castle's door. "The grand duchess will be awaiting you," he said formally.

I'll bet, Nancy thought.

Thanking Pieter, she and George got out of the car. The castle door swung open, and a maid greeted them with a half bow. "Welcome back," she said. "Dinner is just being served. The grand duchess awaits you in the dining room." She took the girls' coats.

"Would you tell her I'll be there in a moment?" Nancy asked. "I need to stop in my room first."

"As you wish," the maid replied. She set off for the dining hall with George following.

Nancy climbed the grand staircase, but instead of going to her bedroom, she made her way quickly along the corridor and descended the stone staircase in the corner tower that was used by servants. At the bottom, Nancy could hear the clatter of pots and pans in the kitchen and the cook moving about. Carefully she peered around the corner. The coast was clear.

Nancy moved into the hall and followed it to the small iron door. Quickly she forced the heavy bolts open and turned the handle. The door opened a crack. A chilly breeze swept past her, and she made out the dark shape of the footbridge and the reflections of light from the castle windows on the water in the moat. Quietly Nancy closed the door, leaving it unlocked. Then she headed back up the servants' stairs to the dining room.

The grand duchess, Emma, and George were seated at the long banquet table. A silver candelabrum burned brightly in the center of the table, its light reflecting off the crystal goblets.

"Sorry I'm late," Nancy said. She couldn't tell from George's expression what, if anything, had been discussed.

"No apologies are necessary," the grand duchess said graciously. "Did you enjoy the club today?"

"The band was great," George answered between bites of roast duckling.

"I understand that my grandchildren did not join you."

"That was entirely Andrei's fault." Emma grimaced. "That's the second car he's drowned in the last three years. The first was his Maserati. You'd think he'd learn."

Clearly, Nancy thought, Emma didn't know that anything had changed. But she wasn't sure about the grand duchess. Either Jaap van der Meer hadn't informed her yet of Merissa's freedom, or she and George were being very neatly set up.

"Where is Andrei?" Nancy asked curiously.

"Still talking to insurance companies, I imagine," the grand duchess replied. "So you spent the entire afternoon at Paradiso?"

Nancy was getting an awful feeling about this. The grand duchess was a little too interested in how they'd spent their day. "Actually," Nancy answered, "we went to a café for pastries afterward."

The elderly aristocrat sent a sharp glance to the untouched food on Nancy's plate. "No wonder you have so little appetite."

Nancy was beginning to feel that the tense meal would never end. As the maid cleared away the plates from the main course, Nancy glanced out the large dining room windows just in time to see the lights of a vehicle entering the castle gates. It circled the courtyard, and she heard it come to a stop outside the great front door.

Nancy's heart pounded. Who had just arrived at the castle? Nancy was willing to lay odds it was Jaap van der Meer, and if the grand duchess didn't already know about Merissa's escape, she was about to find out.

Nancy glanced at George and saw a controlled wariness in her friend's eyes. "This is it," her expression seemed to say. "The trap's been sprung."

The grand duchess was also watching the windows. She stood up, and Nancy had the odd sensation that a mask had just been dropped. There was none of the regal graciousness in her manner now. She eyed Nancy and George with a cold malevolence. "Apparently we have guests arriving," she said. "You must excuse us for a moment. Emma, come with me, please."

Emma looked mystified. "Grandmama—?"

"*Now,* Emma!"

With an apologetic glance at the girls, Emma rose and followed her grandmother out of the dining hall.

Nancy and George were left alone.

Albert Don's car hurtled into the dark country night. Frank realized they were driving along the top of a dike on a paved road.

"This is a different route," Joe said from the backseat just as the Dutch agent turned the car onto a dirt track. Several hundred feet away the great spindly silhouette of an ancient windmill lurked, wreathed by thin, low-lying mist. Don stopped the car.

"We're half a mile from the castle," Albert Don told the Hardys, pointing across the field, where a faint light flickered between trees. "This way we'll approach it from behind."

Twenty minutes later they found themselves on the pebbled road behind the castle. They approached cautiously, waiting in the shadows of leafless shrubs along the edge of the moat. The high castle walls loomed above them on the other side. Light gleamed from a single, high window. Frank could make out the footbridge not far ahead and the doorway in the brick wall. He saw Albert Don wave and step onto the narrow footbridge.

"Let's go," Joe whispered from behind. The Hardys raced forward one at a time. Quickly and quietly they moved across the bridge and squeezed into the doorway. Already the thick castle walls hid them from anyone who might look out.

Frank gripped the cold iron handle and pushed the heavy door. Slowly it swung open, revealing a dimly lit corridor with stone walls. They slipped inside and closed the door behind them. Frank mentally ran through the directions Nancy had given him. He motioned to Joe and Albert Don to follow.

They made their way through the dimly lit passage, avoiding the kitchen, and found the servants' staircase in the corner tower. At the second-floor landing, Frank tried the door. It opened into a narrow, wood-paneled hallway. A dim light glowed in a wall sconce. There was another door at the other end. He signaled Joe and Albert forward, then moved toward it.

They emerged in the second-floor hallway. Frank heard the muffled murmur of voices to his left. With his back pressed against the doorframe, Frank peered around the corner. Light glowed from beneath the tall paneled doors that led to the dining room. He motioned Joe and Albert to go right.

They turned into the tapestry-lined hall that ran down the center of the castle's main wing. Now they were in familiar territory. Frank headed for the library doors.

The luxurious room was almost dark, with only a couple of table lamps with black shades illuminating it. The antique furniture and ancient mirrors were burnished by the dim glow.

Frank went quickly to the fireplace on the right, his eyes searching the detailed carving along the top bookshelf on one side. He saw the goatlike head of a satyr with long, elegantly carved wooden horns precisely in the center. He reached up and gripped the left horn. It turned easily.

There was a momentary stillness in the room, and he was aware of Joe and Albert Don standing behind him. Something inside the wall clicked— the sound of metal on metal. The entire bookcase slid smoothly open like a door.

A dank, musty smell and damp, cold air wafted from the dark opening. Stone steps, cracked and broken, led down into a black abyss.

"It's the entrance to the fifth tower," Joe whispered.

"Let's go," Frank breathed in a voice so low it was barely audible.

"Wait!" Joe had turned to look behind him to make sure no one was following them. Nearby was a marble-topped desk, on which was a leather-bordered blotter and a set of antique crystal inkwells. Joe walked over to it.

Frank and Albert Don looked at each other, puzzled by Joe's sudden interest in the desk.

Joe picked up a filigreed gold mechanical pencil lying on the desk, then walked over to Frank and held it in front of him. It was engraved with the letter *A*. "Does this remind you of something?" Joe asked.

Frank nodded. "The pen in Appel's office. It must have been part of a set."

Albert Don looked puzzled.

"Tell you later," Joe said, quickly replacing the pencil. "Let's go for the gold."

They entered the dusty tower, the glow of their flashlights indicating stone steps descending to unknown depths through low brick arches. The musty odor grew suffocating.

Frank led, the beam from his flashlight bobbing along the brick walls. The steps circled down, at least thirty feet, he estimated, which would put them below the level of the castle's ground floor. Behind him, Joe's and Albert Don's flashlights created monstrous shadows that slithered ahead of him as he descended into the depths of the castle.

"The moat is just on the other side of this wall," Frank said quietly, his flashlight beam weaving up and down on the brick wall. Water seeping through cracks and seams wet the entire wall, and its surface was slick and shiny.

Ten steps below, Frank saw a level stone floor, and the steps ended. With the flashlight he picked out the outline of a stone arch. Crudely spiraled columns had been chiseled into the sides, topped with strange, winged beasts.

"This is amazing!" Albert Don said, gazing at the arch. "These designs are very old. This may be the most ancient part of the castle."

"Let's see what's in there." Joe shone his

flashlight through the arch and stepped over the threshold. He was in a round room, with stone walls. The yellow beam glinted on metal. Millions of dollars' worth of gold ingots were piled neatly in the center of the castle's underground room!

Joe froze as he heard footsteps on the stone steps behind them.

Frank felt his own heart hammering. "Someone's coming!" he said softly. Then he swung around to face the unexpected intruder.

Chapter

Sixteen

F RANK FELT HIS HEART slow to its normal pace as Nancy and George appeared at the foot of the stairs, holding a candelabrum to light their way. The flickering candlelight made their shadows ghostly and huge against the ancient brick walls.

"A car just arrived at the castle," Nancy said breathlessly. "I sneaked partway down the front stairs to find out who it was. It's van der Meer with his two goons and Andrei. We have to get out of here!" Frank moved to one side, revealing the stack of gold bullion.

"The stolen gold!" George said, her voice breathless with awe.

"Let's go!" Frank said. "Before we get trapped down here."

Albert Don grabbed one of the ingots and hefted it in his hand. The edges of the bar were tapered all the way around, and the top bore the distinctive stamped imprint of the Dutch bank. "This is all I need."

They fled up the steps and stepped into the empty library. Joe pushed the bookcase, and the secret door swung closed. Frank raced to the library doors. He ran into the hall with Albert Don behind him, just in time to see the bodyguards rushing toward them.

Frank tackled the stocky one around his knees and knocked him to the floor. Albert Don tackled the second man. Nancy and George slipped out of the library just as Frank and the bodyguard hit the floor. They were locked together in a desperate struggle, rolling across the floor. The bodyguard, who had tremendous strength, managed to pin down Frank.

"Let him go!" George ordered. When the man ignored her, she pushed over the six-foot vase that guarded the library door. The heavy porcelain toppled, striking the bodyguard on the head and smashing into hundreds of pieces.

Frank felt the man's hands, which were now around his neck, suddenly stiffen. Then his opponent lost consciousness. Frank pushed him off and leapt to his feet, scattering broken china everywhere.

Nancy saw Albert Don and the other bodyguard struggling against the enormous tapestry that hung on the wall. She jumped at it, caught hold of one side, and pulled hard. The heavy woven fabric tumbled down.

Joe saw it coming. The bodyguard didn't. Joe grabbed at Albert, pulling him back, while the tapestry crashed on top of the bodyguard, its immense fabric swallowing him.

"Quick!" Joe cried, suddenly grabbing the edge of the one Persian carpet that lined the hall and had no furniture on it. Nancy understood immediately what he was doing and rushed to help.

They threw the carpet over the unconscious bodyguard and rolled him up in it. Albert Don helped Frank roll the other guard in the tapestry.

George raced to the top of the grand staircase and peered down. Van der Meer was pacing anxiously below. There was no sign of the Romanov–von Badens.

She ran back to the others. The bodyguard under the tapestry was still conscious, but his muffled protests were almost inaudible, and his struggles were useless against the heavy fabric that imprisoned him.

"Van der Meer's covering the front staircase," she told them.

"Let's get out the back way," Nancy said. She led them toward the servants' staircase in the tower. They descended the narrow steps quickly in single file.

Frank was just about to step into the corridor on the castle's ground floor when he heard voices in Dutch, the harsh bark of anger and orders.

Quickly he motioned to the others to stop. Then he peered around the corner. He saw Andrei speaking angrily to Pieter in Dutch and then walking toward the door that led to the footbridge.

"Our escape route's gone," Joe whispered quietly in Frank's ear. He was standing beside his brother on the steps.

Frank looked the other way down the corridor. There was another door on the corridor, and if he remembered correctly, it led into the armor room, and then the great hall. If Jaap was still by the grand staircase, Frank knew that they could make it to the front doors unseen, if they were careful. But first they had to get into the armor room without Pieter or Andrei catching them.

Motioning the others to follow, Frank quickly moved into the hall and made for the door. He opened it. The room beyond was in almost complete darkness, but he could make out the tall, vaguely human shapes of armor standing like sentinels. He waved for the others to go through.

Joe saw Nancy and George move into the armor room. He and Albert Don stepped from the stairwell into the corridor and made for the door, just as Pieter stormed around the corner, a rifle in his hand.

Instead of shooting the rifle, Pieter swung it. The stock came down on Don's head, and the Dutch agent crumbled to the stone floor. The force of the blow broke the rifle in two. Instinctively Joe clenched his fist and swung, connecting hard with Pieter's jaw. The surprised chauffeur sagged to the floor and lay still.

Frank rushed back into the hallway, with Nancy and George right behind him.

Joe knelt beside Albert Don. "Albert," he whispered. "You okay?"

The agent was breathing but unconscious. Frank and Nancy quickly knelt and pulled the agent to his feet. With help from Joe and George, they carried him through the door into the armor room.

On the far side of the room a thin line of light glowed under the thick wooden door that led to the great hall. The four friends moved toward it, Albert Don slumped between Frank and Nancy.

Frank opened the door a crack. "We're going to have to make a run for it," he said.

Joe hung back, staring at the paneled doors that led to the drawing room, where the Fabergé eggs were displayed. He felt his muscles tense as the doors swung open.

Emma stood in the opening, her hands clasped nervously in front of her and her cheeks wet from crying. She looked at Joe, her eyes filled with sorrow.

Frank glanced back and saw Emma, too. Was the grand duchess—or Jaap—much farther behind? "Come on, Joe!" he urged.

"We can't stop," Nancy said.

"You go ahead, I'll be right with you," Joe shot back.

Frank hesitated. Nancy and George took Albert Don between them and carried him into the great hall.

"Go!" Joe told his brother. "I'll catch up."

Reluctantly Frank turned and went after the others.

"I don't know what is going on!" Emma said, stepping toward Joe. Her blue eyes searched his, probing for an answer.

Joe looked at her, wanting to be honest but wondering how much he could risk telling her. He reached for her, resting his hands gently on her arms.

"I know you don't know what's going on," he began quietly. "I think you're the only person in the castle I can trust. Emma, that gold that was stolen so many years ago during the war—it never left the castle. It's hidden here, and Jaap van der Meer and your grandmother know about it. They might even have stolen it. Van der Meer is dangerous. He kidnapped Merissa, and now he's after us."

"But why can't you leave my grandmother alone?" Emma sobbed.

"Because whatever happened back then was wrong, Emma. Eight people were slaughtered. And the killing is still going on. You've got to trust me, Emma." Joe started to edge toward the door that led to the great hall. "Let's get out of here. Please don't call for help!"

Emma stared at Joe, her face tormented, and tears streaming down her cheeks.

"Joe, hurry up while the coast is clear!" Frank said from the door.

Emma spun around and slammed the drawing room doors shut behind her. Joe felt his heart skip a beat, then heard Frank call him again. He turned and raced into the great hall.

Nancy and George still carried Albert Don between them and were stepping through the open front door. Frank and Joe ran to their side and took the unconscious agent from them. They heard shouts, followed by footsteps racing through another part of the castle.

Lights from the castle windows glowed across the cobblestones in the courtyard outside. A hundred feet away, freedom beckoned through the open castle gate.

"We left the car on a dirt road half a mile back behind the castle," Joe told Nancy and George.

"Then let's go around the back," George said.

"We don't have time for that," Frank said. "Let's just get into the woods where we can hide until the search eases up."

They started across the courtyard, Frank and Joe running as best they could with an unconscious man draped between them. Nancy and George ran ahead, watching anxiously for any sign of van der Meer or his men. Frank knew that if they could just get beyond the castle walls, they had a chance.

They were almost at the gate when they heard the sound of gears creaking and chains tightening.

George stopped in her tracks and stared at the gate. "The drawbridge is being raised!" she cried. "We're trapped!"

Chapter

Seventeen

Y OU'VE GONE quite far enough," said a distinguished voice behind them.

Nancy turned, not surprised to see Jaap van der Meer and his bodyguards standing at the castle door. The bodyguards looked sullen, she noted, but they had recovered from the fight in the corridor. Moonlight glinted off a silver blade in Jaap's hand. The two guards also held knives. Prince Andrei stood off to the side, looking pale and worried. Behind her, Nancy heard the drawbridge slamming against the stone battlements.

Van der Meer regarded Frank and Joe, who were still supporting Albert between them. "Put him down," van der Meer ordered. Joe and Frank gently lowered Albert to the ground.

Van der Meer turned to the taller guard.

"Search him," he said, pointing to the unconscious man. The guard obeyed. He found the gold bar, which he pocketed. Then he found Albert's revolver, which he handed to van der Meer.

"You almost made it," van der Meer said to the Hardys. He gave a soft laugh and nodded at the unconscious Albert Don. "You will find that it rarely pays to be too heroic."

"That's never been one of your problems, has it?" Frank asked angrily. "Especially on a certain night in 1944 when eight Resistance fighters were executed here and a cache of stolen Dutch gold mysteriously vanished."

Jaap shrugged. "Matter does not 'vanish.' It moves, remains, or is transformed."

"Thanks for the physics lesson," Joe snapped. "Tell us, were you always secretly a Nazi or did you just 'transform' yourself that night when you put on a German uniform?"

"I am a citizen of the Netherlands," Jaap said indignantly. "I worked for the Resistance the entire time our country was occupied. *No one* fought the Nazis harder than I did."

"Then what happened?" Nancy asked.

"Our intelligence told us of the German plan to steal the gold," Jaap answered. "So we disguised ourselves as German soldiers and rerouted it here to the castle for safekeeping."

George shivered under the moonlight. "Too bad it wasn't safe from you."

"You cannot understand what it was like to live under the Occupation," van der Meer replied angrily. "Our people were reduced to stripping clothing from dead bodies. For food we raided garbage cans, and when that wasn't enough, we ate our own cats and dogs. *Everything* was taken from us. For years we had nothing."

"And then you suddenly had a truckful of gold bullion," Nancy said softly. "And you and Appel decided that you weren't about to let it go. So you turned on your fellow Resistance fighters and slaughtered them in the courtyard. It was you and Appel dressed as Nazi officers, wasn't it?"

"There were many executions during the war," Jaap replied evasively.

Joe gave a low whistle. "You really are a piece of work. You killed the people who trusted you and then, still dressed as Nazi officers, you drove the trucks of gold from the castle. But the trucks were empty. The gold was hidden in the tower all along. And you and the Romanov–von Badens here have been living off it ever since."

"Even worse, you invented all these stories about how you and Appel miraculously survived the massacre," Frank said. "You were decorated as heroes for it. Your crime is worse than theft— it's treason and betrayal of the worst kind."

Van der Meer nodded, a cynical smile on his face. "For Americans you are quite intelligent. You've uncovered all my secrets, which, of course, leaves me no choice. In a few short hours you will no longer be a threat to me."

Nancy's pulse began to hammer. The implication was clear. The man was about to kill them.

"Enough talk," van der Meer said briskly. He nodded to his guards, who began to close in on their captives.

Nancy suddenly became aware of Prince Andrei. He was standing completely still and looking shaken. "Andrei," she said, "you heard all of that. Are you just going to stand there and let him kill us?"

Andrei's eyes were panicked. "You must believe me," he said in a pleading tone. "I never knew where the gold came from—or what its history was. Only that I would occasionally take it to Appel for Grandmother, and he would sell it. I had nothing to do with Merissa's disappearance."

"That should give you a clear conscience," Frank retorted. "You didn't abduct your fiancée. You only murdered Appel."

Andrei froze for a moment. Then he shook his head, clearly flustered. "No. I—"

"You dropped your gold pen at the scene of the crime," Joe told him. "You know, the pen engraved with the letter *A*. We assumed the *A* stood for 'Appel'—until Frank noticed the matching gold mechanical pencil in your library tonight. It looked like one of a set, and the other was missing."

"I was in Appel's office earlier in the week," Andrei insisted. "I must have dropped it then."

Nancy's blue eyes widened as she began to put together the final pieces of the puzzle. "The morning that Appel was murdered," she said, "was our first morning here at the castle. You left really early to go into Amsterdam and came back during breakfast. That's what that little business trip into the city was—while we were eating breakfast you went in to kill Appel."

"No, I went to Amsterdam to see about some investments and—"

"Oh, Andrei, stop these silly denials," van der Meer said impatiently. "It doesn't matter what they know. They won't live to tell anyone."

Nancy ignored van der Meer's interruption. It was still hard for her to believe Andrei had committed murder. She turned to the handsome young aristocrat. "Why would you want to kill Appel? What did he ever do to you?"

Andrei stared back at her, silent.

Furious, Nancy turned on Jaap van der Meer. "You know why Appel was killed, don't you?" she demanded. "In fact, you're probably the one who ordered the murder."

"It couldn't be helped," van der Meer said. "Appel was getting nervous, guilty about what we did years ago. He refused to broker any more of the bullion, and he was threatening to go to the police."

"Johannes would have ruined everything," Andrei added in a helpless tone. "My family, our money—we had no choice."

Nancy decided to try one last appeal. "Andrei, now you *do* have a choice. You know the truth about Jaap and the horrors he's responsible for. Help us!"

For a moment Andrei gazed at her, clearly trying to sort through a barrage of conflicting emotions. Nancy saw a flash of sympathy in his dark eyes. Then a cold and implacable expression replaced it, and she knew their fate was sealed. Without another glance, the prince turned his back on them and walked away.

"A very good friend, that one," van der Meer said in a dry tone. "His loyalties will always lie with his money. Andrei!" he called sharply.

The prince stopped in his tracks but did not turn.

"I have further need of you," van der Meer said. "You will help us until we leave the grounds."

Like an obedient servant, the prince walked back across the cobblestones, his pale face empty of emotion.

One of the bodyguards reached down and removed a knife from beneath his pants leg. He held it out to Andrei, who took it without question.

Van der Meer signaled almost imperceptibly to his men. Nancy gasped as her left arm was suddenly twisted behind her, and the point of a knife was brought to her throat.

"I suggest you come very quietly," van der Meer said. "Unless you want to watch your friends die."

Frank, Joe, and George, she saw, were being similarly held; Jaap and his men, acting simultaneously, had captured the entire group without a struggle. It had happened so smoothly that Nancy realized they must have performed this type of maneuver before. Even Andrei played his part smoothly, holding a knife on George. Joe struggled against the bigger of the two bodyguards, until his arms were pinned to his sides.

"Let's go," van der Meer said curtly. "We've wasted enough time."

The four Americans were prodded to the side of an old truck. At a signal from van der Meer, they were tied up with ropes and tossed unceremoniously into its back. Seconds later Albert Don, similarly bound and still unconscious, joined them.

Nancy looked at him with a worried glance. "He's been out for a while now. I hope he's okay."

"He may be better off than we are," Joe said. He had just heard the sound of the drawbridge being lowered. Then the truck started up. "Somehow I don't think this is going to be fun." He struggled for a minute with the ropes at his wrists and ankles, then gave a helpless shrug. "I was hoping they didn't really know how to tie a knot."

Nancy lurched to the side as the truck peeled out of the castle's courtyard. With some difficulty she righted herself. "At least they didn't gag us," she pointed out.

"Which probably means that the route we're

taking will be all back roads where whatever noise we make won't matter," Frank said.

Joe grimaced. "Thank you for sharing that cheerful thought with us."

George wriggled around so that her back was against Nancy's. "Let's try to work on each other's knots," she suggested.

Nancy probed with her fingers until she found the knots that bound George's hands. But her own ropes were tied too tightly to allow her enough movement to free her friend. Her fingers were almost numb from a lack of blood.

"This isn't working," George said a short time later.

"Let me try," said Frank. But though they all attempted to untie one another, they were all bound too tightly to succeed.

"It's no good," Frank admitted. "All we're doing is getting rope burns."

And freezing, Nancy added silently. Although the Hardys and Albert Don wore jackets, she was dressed in jeans and a sweater, as was George. The cold night wind cut through the meager protection of their clothing.

Sighing, Nancy leaned back against the side of the truck. Don't panic, she told herself. There has to be a way out of this. We're not going to give up hope.

Across from her, Joe cracked an irreverent smile. "Anyone for a round of 'A Hundred Bottles of Beer on the Wall'?"

* * *

As the truck came to a halt Frank peered at the luminous face on Joe's watch. "It's only been a half hour since we left the castle," he said.

"Are you sure?" George asked. "It feels as if we've been riding forever."

"Positive. Wherever we are, we're not all that far."

"Yeah, but Holland's a small country. If you miss your bus stop here, you end up in Germany," Frank kidded.

The door to the back of the truck opened. Jaap's thugs climbed in, each of them holding cloth rags in their hands. Without a word they calmly and methodically blindfolded the Americans, as well as Albert Don, even though he was unconscious.

Then the truck started up again. This time Frank had no idea how long they traveled. He knew only that when they finally stopped, he could hear the sound of water lapping against the shore, and smell the tangy saltwater scent of the sea.

Another odor was mixed in with that of the saltwater, something he couldn't identify at first. Then he realized it was the heavy, acrid odor of coal.

The truck backed up, and then the engine was cut. Again Frank heard the sound of truck doors opening, and their captors climbed into the back. Then he and the others were thrown roughly over the tailgate onto a floor of some kind.

Frank felt the rope around his ankles being cut.

Arms pulled him to his feet, and a rough shove sent him walking straight ahead. Then someone pushed him, and he stumbled down a short flight of stairs.

He heard three other sets of footsteps—Joe, Nancy, and George joining him—then a thud that could only have been Albert Don's body being dropped beside him. Above them, a door slammed shut and a lock slid into place.

"Where are we?" Frank asked aloud.

"I don't know," Nancy replied. "But there's a wooden floor beneath us."

"Which is now slowly moving," Joe pointed out. "And you can hear water lapping against the wood on the other side. From the sea air and all, I'll bet you anything we're on a boat."

"A coal barge!" Frank exclaimed. "I knew I recognized the smell!"

"What's that scratching sound?" George demanded, her voice alarmed.

"Rats," Joe said casually.

"Terrific," George murmured.

Frank heard Albert Don moan. In a drowsy voice, barely more than a mumble, the Dutch agent asked, "What happened? Where are we?" He groaned with pain when he tried to move his head.

Frank breathed a sigh of relief. "Glad you're awake. You almost missed the fun. Van der Meer and his men tied us up. We think we're on a coal barge somewhere."

Another sound interrupted his explanation.

"That's weird," Nancy said. "It sounds like running water."

"It *feels* like running water," Joe howled as a wave of ice-cold water rushed across the floor, soaking his shoes and the seat of his pants.

"And it's getting deeper," Frank added grimly, feeling the icy water spread, numbing his skin where his clothes were wet.

"They've opened the plugs," Albert Don said. "They're sinking the boat."

"How do you know?" George asked.

"Considering that we are being flooded, it's a reasonable deduction," the agent replied.

"But why would anyone sink the boat unless they wanted to—" Nancy left the last part of her question unasked. She remembered what the taxi driver had said on their first ride into Amsterdam—no one could survive more than three minutes in such cold water. Van der Meer wanted them to die of exposure, and if that didn't work, they would probably drown.

"I had it all wrong," George said in an odd, strained voice. "The rats weren't coming in here to get us. They were scratching like mad because they were trying to get out."

Frank shivered as the ice-cold water continued to wash across the floor and soak his pants. It was growing deeper every second. It was only a matter of time before the ship sank and they drowned.

Chapter

Eighteen

J OE FELT the barge sink farther, and the angle of the floor grow steeper. Water rushed down the wooden planks from high end to low. The wooden boat creaked and groaned in the darkness around them.

Joe pushed himself up along the slanted floor to the highest point he could reach. "Up this way!" he yelled to the others. He heard someone grunt and push along the floor.

"I'm up here with you!" Nancy called from nearby.

"And me," said George.

"The water's coming in fast," Frank said, pulling himself along the steeply inclined floor toward Joe's voice. "Where's Albert?"

"I'm all right," the Dutch man answered.

Joe heard the wooden planks groan. The boat jerked and listed even more. A wave nibbled at his running shoes, then ebbed. He heard something rattling and felt several small hard objects tumble past his hands. Almost without thinking, he grabbed one with his fingers.

It felt like a rock. He turned it with his fingers. It was a big round lump of something that had one sharp edge. "Frank, you said you thought this was a coal barge?"

"That's right," Frank's voice came back from the pitch-blackness.

"I think I just found a piece of coal, and we're going to get out of here," Joe said excitedly. He backed against the hull and wedged the hard lump of coal between his hands, the rope, and the wood. The sharp, jagged edge of the rock pressed into the rope. Slowly and carefully Joe started sawing back and forth.

Another wrenching grind of wood against wood warned Joe when the boat dipped again, and he froze. The chunk of coal didn't fall. If it did, Joe knew the game was over.

"Hurry!" Nancy told him.

"You're not kidding," Frank muttered in the darkness. "If this barge sinks any more, there's no way we'll be able to stay out of the water."

"I'm halfway through," Joe shot back, redoubling his effort. He pressed the rope harder against the raw edge of rock and pulled with his arms. The rope split.

"I'm out of here!" Joe cried. He pulled off his

blindfold, then reached into the darkness and found Frank. He removed his brother's blindfold. Then quickly moving his arms down his brother's body, Joe found the thick rope that bound his hands and untied the knots. Frank gave a huge sigh of relief when his hands were freed.

"Find the door," Joe told him. "I'll get to the others." He found Nancy next, then moved on to Albert Don while Nancy freed George. Already the barge was listing so badly it was impossible not to slide into the cold water.

"The door's here!" Frank shouted. He could feel the icy waves rising over his ankles, splashing against his knees.

"The water's r-r-rising f-f-faster," George said, her teeth chattering.

Frank gripped the handle and pulled. It didn't budge. He balled his fist and slammed it against the wood. The door was solid and obviously securely bolted on the outside. He threw himself against it as hard as he could. The wood shuddered, but barely. The freezing water was now swirling around his knees.

"Joe, help me," Frank called into the darkness. "The door's bolted on the outside. Our only hope is to bash it down."

Joe scrambled up the steps, splashing as he went. "Let's do it," he said when he felt Frank's presence beside him.

Suddenly they heard clumping sounds on the other side of the door.

"Footsteps!" Joe said, cutting the silence with a loud whisper. "Someone's unlocking the door!"

The door was thrown open, and Ot Schrijver, the castle groundskeeper, stood in the opening, his craggy face illuminated by the light from an oil lantern. Seawater swirled around his high rubber boots.

"Get out before she sinks," Ot said sharply. "We have no time to waste."

He turned, and Nancy and the others followed him. Frank had been right—they had been imprisoned on a rotting barge, a long, wide boat with a flat bottom and low cabin. It listed badly, and the seawater was already sweeping over one side of the stern.

The barge had been anchored beside a wide canal somewhere in the Dutch countryside. A lane ran along it, bordered by an even row of leafless trees.

Nancy wrapped her arms around herself and tried to stop her teeth from chattering. They were all soaking wet from the flooded hold, and the outside temperature had to be somewhere below freezing. She didn't even want to think about the wind-chill factor. It would be amazing if they made it through the night without getting pneumonia.

"I have a van nearby," Ot said curtly. "You will be able to warm yourselves there."

"Not before we get some answers," Nancy said. She still wasn't sure she trusted Ot

Schrijver. "You've been sabotaging the castle. Why should we trust you?"

"The sabotage was not directed at you," Schrijver told her calmly. "It was meant to frighten the grand duchess." He frowned at her. "You will all freeze to death. My van is on the road, and it is warm. You can ask your questions there, and I will not drive away until you are satisfied."

"Deal," Nancy agreed.

Moments later the six of them crowded into Ot Schrijver's van. Nancy waited until he'd switched on the heater before asking, "Why were you trying to terrorize the grand duchess?"

"I was ten years old in 1944," he answered, "when Jaap van der Meer and the grand duchess were responsible for my parents' death. My name was not Schrijver then. It was Blankert."

Nancy caught George's eye with a knowing look. It was the name from the document in the drawer in Ot's cottage. He was the little boy in the photograph!

The man continued. "My parents were both Resistance fighters, and I was very proud of them. Like all ten-year-olds at the time, I dreamed of helping their cause.

"One night my parents left the house very late. I knew they were going out on a mission, and I decided that for once I would not be left behind. We were always hiding from the Nazis, so I'd become very good at making myself invisible.

When I wanted, even my parents could not find me.

"That night I sneaked onto their truck and secretly went with them to the castle. I saw the gold being unloaded and watched the grand duchess take custody of it. And then," he continued in a flat, quiet voice, "I saw my parents lined up against the wall and shot. I also saw the faces of their murderers—Appel and van der Meer. I have lived my entire life with this secret."

"Why didn't you tell someone?" Joe asked.

"No one would have taken the word of a schoolboy against that of Jaap van der Meer," Ot Schrijver replied bitterly. "I knew I had to expose them. My entire life, I've plotted. Three years ago I became the castle groundskeeper, watching them, looking for the evidence I needed."

"Then you knew the gold never left the castle," Joe said.

"Of course," Schrijver answered. "I saw it carried inside. But I didn't know where it was, and that was the proof I needed to convince the authorities."

"That's why you were tapping on the castle walls," Nancy said.

Schrijver smiled. "There is a tower in the castle that has no normal entrance. I have been trying for a long time to find it—with no luck."

"But why the scare tactics at the castle?" Joe demanded. "The blood in the courtyard—"

"The blue china monkey," George added.

"I wanted to scare the grand duchess, to create tensions so that perhaps she would confess or make mistakes that would help me find the hiding place of the gold. I changed the sails on the windmill every day to match the signals used on the night the gold was stolen. I sent her the blue monkey to remind her of the tavern where the Resistance fighters met. I put the blood on the courtyard wall. If I must live with the past, then so must she," he finished in a stern voice.

"Did you lock us in the windmill?" George asked.

Schrijver looked at her and nodded. "To scare you off. I knew your friend had disappeared, and I suspected that van der Meer and the duchess were responsible. I thought you were in much greater danger than even you knew. Yet you were suspicious of me. I was afraid you would tell the duchess I was behind the sabotage."

"I did," Nancy said with a wry smile. "She didn't believe me."

"She is a very arrogant woman," Schrijver said softly. "I did not mean to harm you, only to secure your safety."

"How did you get the name Schrijver?" Frank asked.

"The Schrijvers were the couple who adopted me after my parents were killed. They were kind to me, and so I took their name."

"That explains just about everything," Frank concluded, looking at Nancy and Joe.

"Except how you found us on the boat," Joe said.

Schrijver turned to face him. "Emma came to me in my cottage. She told me that you were in trouble and begged me to follow Jaap's truck to see that you were all right."

Joe smiled. "I knew I could trust her."

Schrijver gave him a strange look. "This a very serious thing Emma did. To save your lives she betrayed her entire family. This night will change everything for Emma. I hope you appreciate what she risked for you."

"Please," Albert Don said, "you must take us to a phone. I want to get police backup out to the castle now. If the gold is still there, the Dutch government has the right to reclaim it."

"What do you mean *if* the gold is still there?" Joe asked. "We saw it a few hours ago."

"If I were Jaap and someone had discovered my secret cache of stolen gold," Albert said, "I would move the gold as quickly as possible."

Ot Schrijver started up the van and drove onto a paved road. A few miles farther on, he pulled up at a public phone in the square of a small village. The Dutch intelligence agent made his call.

"Now," Albert Don instructed Schrijver, "take us to the castle."

To Nancy the ride back seemed nearly as endless as the ride away from it had been. What if they didn't get there in time? What if they found the secret tower empty, with Jaap and the Romanov–von Badens gone?

At last they neared the castle. From the road they could see that the high iron gate was closed. There was no sign of Albert's police backup anywhere.

"Stop here," Albert ordered. "I'll go in on foot."

"We'll follow you," Nancy said.

"That's impossible," Albert told her. "I cannot involve civilians."

"They took your gun," Frank reminded him. "You're unarmed, and we're the only backup you have."

The Dutch agent looked reluctant but did not object. "I have an idea," Ot Schrijver said. "If you go on foot to the castle, you will surely be spotted. However, they do not suspect me. If all of you stay out of sight, I can drive through the gates and let you off in the back courtyard. They will think I am alone."

Albert Don protested. "Mijnheer Schrijver, I cannot involve you. You have saved our lives. I cannot risk yours."

"It would be my pleasure," Schrijver replied. "For many years I have waited for this day. Now," he said firmly, "if you will all please get down . . ."

Without a word the entire group quickly got down on the floor of the van.

Schrijver drove across the bridge, then stopped at the iron gates. He got out of the van, opened the gates, then drove across the drawbridge, past the front courtyard to the back of the castle.

"Now," he said, stepping out of the van, "you can get out. But be very careful. I saw no one, but the truck is there, and the castle gates are open."

Everyone thanked Schrijver as they got out of the van. Keeping to the shadows, Albert Don and the four teens made their way to the front of the castle.

Nancy caught her breath at the sight that greeted them in the courtyard. Light blazed through the castle windows, and the great doors were wide open. Van der Meer, his men, and Andrei were carrying the stolen gold bullion from the castle and loading it into the back of the truck!

Chapter

Nineteen

Albert Don pulled his badge from his pocket and stepped forward into the castle courtyard. Frank and Joe fanned out on both sides of him while Nancy, George, and Ot Schrijver remained a step behind.

"I demand that you surrender!" Don shouted, holding up his badge.

Jaap van der Meer, Andrei, and the bodyguards froze and turned. With a loud clunk the gold bars fell heavily to the cobblestones. Frank saw van der Meer blanch as if he were seeing ghosts.

"You are like vermin," the traitor snarled. "Impossible to get rid of." He turned to his bodyguards. "Get them," he ordered. "And this time kill them immediately."

Before Nancy could stop him, Ot Schrijver ran past her. "You murderer!" the groundskeeper screamed. "I will avenge the deaths of Max and Elsa Blankert!"

He threw himself at van der Meer, who dodged to one side. The short, stocky bodyguard reached down and grabbed a gold bar from the cobblestones where it had fallen.

Joe raced forward to stop him, but it was too late. The bodyguard smashed the heavy gold bar against the side of Schrijver's head. The man stumbled. His knees buckled, and his eyes rolled up into his head. He fell to the ground, unconscious.

Joe saw the bodyguard turn in his direction. He raised his elbow to block him, but the thug jabbed from the left with an undercut. The ham-size fist pounded into Joe's stomach and knocked him breathless. He doubled over in pain.

Frank and George saw Joe go down and raced to help. George grabbed the guard's arm just as he threw a punch at Frank. Frank slugged him in the jaw and grabbed his other arm. In seconds they had his arms twisted behind his back. Frank rifled through the man's pockets until he found the knife.

Nancy saw the other bodyguard reach under his pant leg and pull his knife from an ankle sheath. Before she could move, Albert Don tackled him, knocking him down. The knife flew into the air and skittered along the cobblestones. The two men locked arms and struggled. Nancy jumped into the fray, aiming a high karate kick to the goon's back. Don slipped from his attacker's grip, and the man went down face first. Nancy immediately sat on him.

Jaap van der Meer watched the melee until his bodyguards went down. Then, taking Albert Don's revolver out of his pocket, he started backing steadily toward the cab of the truck, glancing around the courtyard for an avenue of escape. There was only one: the drawbridge across the moat.

Suddenly there was a commotion at the castle door. Emma ran from the great hall, her face stained by tears. Not far behind her, the grand duchess pursued her granddaughter.

"No, Emma!" the old woman cried.

"Stop!" Emma shouted. "I've called the police!"

Prince Andrei, cowering by the castle steps, looked horrified. He walked toward his sister. "You don't know what you're doing!" he cried angrily.

"I have no time for family arguments!" Jaap shouted. Jumping forward, he grabbed Emma, pulled her away from the castle, and put the gun to her throat.

Everyone froze.

"Don't try to stop me," Jaap growled. He backed toward the cab of the truck with Emma firmly imprisoned in his arms.

The bodyguard on the ground snorted a triumphant laugh. With a sweep of his arms he pushed Nancy aside. She fell back on the cobblestones while he rose to his knees, casually brushing off his clothes. He looked at Nancy as if he was going to enjoy killing her.

"Let him go!" van der Meer ordered Frank and George. The other bodyguard yanked his arms away from them. With a contemptuous look he joined his colleague, collecting their knives on the way.

Jaap pushed Emma through the driver's door into the truck, keeping his eyes steadily on the Hardys and Nancy Drew.

"If you try to stop me, you will never see Emma again!" he shouted. He pushed his hostage across the seat and climbed behind the wheel.

"Give up the girl now!" Albert Don shouted. "You'll never get away with this!"

Van der Meer ignored him. He looked at the bodyguards who stood near the castle steps. Their knives glinted in the golden light that streamed from the mullioned windows.

"Kill them all," he ordered. He looked at Andrei, who had moved to his grandmother's side. "You help them. You deserve to get your hands dirty for all the money you've gone through."

Joe fought for a deep breath of air and tried to ignore the agonizing ache in his stomach. With Frank's help he tried to rise. He thought of Emma and shook his head to clear the dizziness.

"Andrei!" Emma screamed to her brother. "Help me, please help me!"

Andrei watched, his face blank and his eyes filled with fear. He made no move.

"She's your sister!" Nancy shouted at him. "Are you going to let that monster take her?"

Andrei looked at Nancy helplessly. His mouth opened and then shut, as if he were incapable of speech.

"Forget it," Frank called to Nancy. "He's a murderer. He's already killed once."

Jaap van der Meer started up the truck.

"No!" the grand duchess screamed. She started walking as fast as she could toward the truck. "Let her go, I beg you. Emma has nothing to do with this!"

Joe saw van der Meer sneer at the elderly aristocrat. The truck slowly began to move forward. Joe realized that van der Meer was unfamiliar with driving the vehicle. A plan began to form in his mind.

"You will not take my grandchild!" the grand duchess cried. She tried to run but was too old to move quickly. Nancy saw the old woman's chest heaving as she gasped for air. Suddenly her face was shot with terrible pain. She turned white as a sheet and clutched at her chest.

"My heart!"

Before Nancy could step forward to catch her, the grand duchess stiffened. Slowly she sank to her knees. Then she pitched forward and collapsed facedown on the cobblestones.

"Grandmama!" Emma screamed inside the cab. The truck turned in a large, reckless arc to head for the drawbridge. Then it sputtered and stalled.

Suddenly, from beyond the castle walls, Nancy heard sirens. Red and blue lights flashed on the other side of the moat, and police cars screeched to a halt.

"They're surrounding the grounds!" Nancy shouted. The bodyguards hesitated, glancing around the courtyard.

"Surrender," Nancy told them. "There's no escape now!"

Van der Meer's men looked at each other, their expressions admitting their defeat. Their weapons fell from their hands and clattered on the cobblestones.

"Cover me, Frank!" Joe cried, running toward the truck. He saw van der Meer's panic-stricken face behind the windshield as he started up the truck again. Emma crouched in terror against the door on the passenger side. Joe knew he didn't have much time, but there was a chance he could cut Jaap off before he reached the castle gate.

Spurred by his brother's sudden move, Frank looked around. His eyes lit on the gold bars where they had fallen, not far from Schrijver's unconscious body. Frank scooped up one of the heavy metal bars and flung it at the driver's-side window as the truck sped past.

The glass splintered like a spiderweb and disintegrated. In panic van der Meer braked, just as a police car cruised through the castle gate with its lights flashing. The truck narrowly avoided a head-on collision by veering sideways toward Joe.

Joe saw his chance. He jumped for the door, his fingers closing around the handle, and pulled it open. With his other arm he grabbed Emma. The police car had cleared the gate, and the truck began to accelerate again.

Wrapping his arms around the frightened princess, Joe leapt with her from the truck. The truck careened away from him, and he landed painfully on his side, protecting Emma and cushioning their fall by rolling on the cobblestones.

"The truck's out of control!" Nancy shouted, running toward Joe and Emma.

A fender scraped against one of the stone posts that stood on either side of the castle gates. Metal ripped, sending out a fusillade of bright orange sparks. The truck swerved at the drawbridge. Jaap van der Meer sailed over the edge and into the moat, disappearing in an enormous splash of cold, gray water.

"So when are you two going to come back to Amsterdam for a real visit?" Merissa asked Nancy and George. Two days later the three of them were standing at a crowded gate at Schiphol Airport along with Emma and the Hardys. Frank and Joe had managed to get on the same flight back to the United States.

George glanced at Nancy and smiled. "Maybe when it's warmer out?"

"I'd love to see Holland in the springtime."

"That's the best time of year," Merissa agreed. "I'd love to show you around when all the tulips are in bloom."

"Oh," George said, reaching into her pocket. "I have something of yours." She held out the gold earring.

Merissa smiled. "Thanks. I can't believe an earring helped save my life."

"Are you going to be all right?" George asked her friend.

"Fine," Merissa said. "The hardest part was learning the truth about Andrei—" She stopped as she saw Emma's lip tremble.

The young princess had been subdued ever since the recent events at the castle. Nancy didn't blame her. Her grandmother was dead, and her brother was in jail for murder. Still, Nancy had been impressed with her resilience. Emma was staying with a friend in Amsterdam and making arrangements to live with cousins in France until she was old enough to take her place as heiress to the Romanov–von Baden estate.

"I was crazy about him," Merissa finished quietly. "I've never had as much fun with anyone as I had with Andrei."

"He cared for you, too," Emma said. "Only he cared about money more."

"But you didn't," Joe said.

Emma blushed. "Let's talk about other things." She turned to Joe. "When are *you* coming back to the Netherlands?"

Joe gazed at the young princess with his heart in his eyes. "I don't know when I'll get back," he told her. "But I will. I promise. And I'll write, in the meantime." He smiled at her. "You could come visit us, too, you know. Our house isn't exactly grand or anything, but—"

Emma laughed. "I didn't expect you to live in a castle."

"Are you going to be all right on your own?" Joe asked her.

"Yes," Emma told him, her voice sure and confident.

"Don't worry," Merissa said. "As long as Emma's in Amsterdam, she and I will look out for each other."

An airline employee announced that the plane was boarding, and the friends hugged and said goodbye. Nancy, George, and the Hardys boarded the plane.

"So," Frank said in a satisfied tone when they were settled into their seats. "The stolen gold has been returned to the government of the Netherlands, Jaap van der Meer is in custody, charged with wartime treason, and Ot Schrijver has avenged his murdered parents at last."

"Plus we rescued Merissa," George reminded

him. "In fact, if it hadn't been for Merissa, none of this might have happened."

"That old castle sure had its share of secrets, didn't it?" said Joe.

Nancy gazed out the window for one last glimpse of the Netherlands. "Case closed," she said with satisfaction.